SON OF THE BLACK CHALICE

By
MILTON LESSER

I0616911

ARMCHAIR FICTION
PO Box 4369, Medford, Oregon 97504

HATED AND HUNTED ACROSS SPACE...

It had been twenty-five years since John Hastings, Sr. first found the Chalice. Only a small number of beings in the whole of the Solar System were chosen to benefit from the power of this amazing discovery, and the ever-growing discord that arose from the ranks of the "unworthy" had become a decidedly dangerous thing.

In this engaging sequel to "Secret of the Black Planet," John Hastings, Jr., hated and hunted by many, looks for answers to his origins. With the help of the Japanese-Venusian half-breed, Suuki, and the vivacious Susan Bentley, young Hastings is determined to put an end to the hostilities facing his friends and family. His amazing quest soon takes him on a journey across the galaxy in search of answers that only the creators of the Black Chalice can ultimately provide.

FOR A SECOND COMPLETE NOVEL, TURN TO PAGE 121

CAST OF CHARACTERS

JOHNNY HASTINGS, JR.

Tired of the combative and resentful nature of the valley throngs he went in search of answers—at peril to his life.

SUSAN BENTLEY

She was lovely, young, and bold—a much-needed asset to the mountain refuge; her passion knew no bounds.

SUUKI

It was his Venusian genius that solved the dilemma of how to get the Children of the Chalice out into the stars.

TIMMONS

He was determined to destroy the Children. For he was not part of the superhuman race...and that was unacceptable.

JOHN HASTINGS, SR.

On the Black Asteroid he had found the Chalice, but was fear and segregation to be his only legacy?

CONDAN

An ancestor of the original superman, a scientist no less. This was the man the struggling descendants had been searching for.

High up on the slopes of the Sierra Nevada Mountains, so high that it is crisply cool even in summer, there is a city. It is a new city and a beautiful one, but people shun—except every once in a while when the rabble came up from the valleys below to hurl their stones. Then the dwellers in the city retreat behind their bolted doors and wait with fear while the angry mobs start the long trek down and back to their valleys. The dwellers in the city have learned to live with fear, for they are Children of the Chalice.

There is on Venus also such a city, and one on Mars. There are hamlets for the Children of the Chalice on the Jovian Moons. But not of the Children live in the reecommended places…

CHAPTER ONE

"I see her, Mark. Oh, Mark, here comes Susan!"

The woman, whose name was Hannah Bentley, stood shivering near the window, squinting out into the gathering gloom. Night on Mars carries on its quick black wings a terrible cold, even in Syrtis Major City, the capital.

"Then come away from the window," Mark Bentley told his wife. "If you stay, Susan will know you were watching, and she'll know you were worried."

"Who's worried? Susan can take care of herself, Mark Bentley."

"You're worried. Now come away from that window."

Hannah Bentley backed away from the thick glass, and then they could hear Susan inserting her key in the lock. A blast of frigid air swept in with Susan from the cold streets outside and the girl had to lean all her weight against the door to shut it.

"Hul-lo," she said, unzipping her furs.

"Her eye, Mark… Look at her eye. The poor thing—"

"I'm all right." Susan eluded her mother's embrace. "I just got into a fight, that's all."

"Your eye is blackened."

"Well, you should see them. Two of them, two boys. I won, Mama."

Mark Bentley nodded. "Of course you won. You're of the Chalice."

"But it isn't right, Mark. It isn't right that an eighteen-year-old girl should have to fight like a boy."

"She's of the Chalice." He always said it like that, Hannah Bentley knew, as if it were the answer to everything.

Susan blew on her hands to warm them. She had long and graceful hands, and they were like the rest of her. Tall and lithe, blossoming only recently into young womanhood. She was beautiful, and her mother had never been anything but plain. Her father was big and work-hardened, but homely. Perhaps the Chalice was responsible for that, too, for Susan Bentley's beauty.

"I don't care, Mark. Susan is a woman now and if that has to happen every time she goes off to visit a friend on the other side of town—"

"What can we do?"

"We can move out of Syrtis Major, that's what. To one of the Chalice Cities, where we belong."

"What? Segregated like that as if—as if we weren't human? Now you, Hannah, you're human…"

"So are you, Mark. You and Susan. Probably, you're more than human. But people don't understand that."

"They hate us," Susan cried. "They hate us because we're better than they are. We're stronger and we live longer and we don't get hurt much and, if we're second generation, we're beautiful. Well, I hate them too."

"You mustn't say that, child."

"I can say what I want, I'm not a child any more. I hate them!"

* * *

John Hastings knew that, twenty-five years before, his father had walked this same path. His father, the first John Hastings, had blasted down upon the Black Asteroid, had been amazed that the place had air and warmth and Earth-normal gravity. Nor had he known that the Chalice awaited him—awaited his coming for countless eons—deep within the bowels of the artificial world.

John Hastings, the son, knew what to expect. But even then, his journey had been a dangerous one. Half the Solar System's military might was clustered in space around the black globe but, miraculously, he'd slipped through the circle of steel and flame. His feet click-clacked briskly on the smooth, hard surface, and he felt a wild triumph welling up within him.

The Black Asteroid. And the Chalice...

He found the door, marked off in phosphorescent white; he fingered the stud of smooth rock and then he pressed it.

Silence for the space of two heartbeats. Then a vague grinding sound, as some hidden mechanism deep within the small world began to function. In a moment, the door slid back. John Hastings walked down the stairs slowly, almost reverently. This was the place. It was here that he had received his birthright, and although the people hated him and his kind, he knew he was more than human. In that knowledge was a certain comfort, for he realized that the first true man must have been shunned and hated like this by his gnarled, hairy fellows.

The utter silence of deep space entered the crypt with him. Nothing stirred. Nothing moved. But the wall glowed with an unknown source of light, and in the center of the room stood the Chalice.

It wasn't black, not really. Only the artificial world was black, and from that the Chalice had received its name. It did not matter. Not even the Chalice mattered. John Hastings sought what lay beyond the Chalice—if anything.

If anything—

There had to be *something*. He'd gambled his life on that, and ultimately he knew, the life of his kind might depend on what he found.

On the walls he could see the ancient murals, which some said had been painted there before the coming of man. Yet the murals showed men and the men stood near a spaceship—and there were men of Venus and Mars as well as of the Earth. Then, long ago—before the fifth planet had burst asunder to form the asteroid belt—the murals had been painted, but by whom? By other men, or so the theories said, by other men who had come before us and planted the seed for us and then departed.

And *surely* they must have left something behind with which to reap the harvest.

John Hastings looked, and found—nothing. There was the Chalice and the bank upon bank of machinery, which yielded power to it. There were the murals and there was the silence. But that was all. Nothing else. The murals were vivid. Over the ages their coloring somehow had not faded, and they were truly tri-dimensional, although when he ran his hand over them, he found the surface flat.

But nothing else...

Wearily, he trudged back toward the stairway. His right foot was on the first step when something jarred the small world.

John Hastings stumbled, fell to hands and knees. When he got to his feet he knew that another spaceship had landed on the Black Asteroid, and he did not have to stretch his imagination to suspect that those within it were hostile.

He eased a blaster from its pouch, crept slowly up the stairs. There were nine of them, he knew. His father had said that nine steps led down to the Chalice. Footsteps struck sharply against the stone, the sound of many men running.

John Hastings peered out. Instantly, something streaked by his head and formed a trickle of melted rock behind him. He ducked quickly back into the crypt, heard a harsh voice:

"Come out of there. Come out of there or we'll come in after you."

*   *   *

"WHAT DO you think you're doing, Susan?"

"You can see for yourself. I'm packing."

"Your father wants to stay here in Syrtis Major. He wants us to stay with him."

"We do not belong in Syrtis Major, Dad and me. You—"

"Oh, then you think I belong. I'm not one of you. Well, I'm not. But I love you, Susan, and I'm your mother."

"I'm sorry. I didn't mean it that way. Dad can stay if he wants. You *should* stay, you wouldn't like it living among the Children. But I'm getting out."

"Susan."

"I'm a woman now. You said so yourself. I want to go where I can be happy, I can't be happy here."

Susan snapped her valise shut with finality. "They hate me," she said. "So I guess I've learned to hate them back. Tell Dad—I didn't want to say goodbye to him. You worry all the time on the outside, Mama. But he worries inside, and that's worse."

"I'll tell him."

"And I'll write to you, Mama—after I'm settled. I don't know where. Here on Mars maybe, or in the Sierra Nevada Mountains on Earth."

Hannah Bentley said nothing. She crossed the room and embraced her daughter. There was so much she wanted to say, so much that the long, aching years had piled up for her to say. But her tongue felt stiff and swollen and suddenly her mouth was very dry. She watched her daughter leave, then ran to the window and stood there a long time until the fur-garbed figure faded slowly from sight.

It was only then that Hannah Bentley began to cry.

* * *

John Hastings crouched at the bottom step. Once a head had appeared briefly above him, but he'd snapped off a quick beam with his blaster, and the head had ducked back out of sight. He couldn't remain in the crypt indefinitely, but he was in no hurry to have them sear him with their weapons. He knew he would take a lot of killing, for a Child of the Chalice did not die easily. But they could hurt him and that was the same thing. He'd be captured and Government would throw the book at him for invading the crypt.

He fired another beam from his blaster to let them know he was still there then he walked back into the crypt itself. Somewhere in there was a central lighting system for the artificial world, and if he could find that and damage it, he might have a chance to return to his ship in darkness. He knew it was hopeless, however. No one understood the machinery within the crypt, and he might as well be looking for a needle in a haystack on the dark side of Pluto.

After a time he gave it up. The banks of machinery were encased completely in smooth, gleaming metal. He could not make head or tail out of them, he was only wasting time. He shrugged, stalked back to the nine stairs.

"Hello out there!"

"We hear you."

"You the police?"

"Damned right. Come on out, wise guy."

"Listen, this crypt is important, isn't it?"

"What do you think?"

"I know it is. Government has decided not to use it any more, but they don't want it destroyed. Right?"

"Yeah."

"Okay. I'm coming out. But I've set a baby atomic down here," John Hastings lied, "and if you lay a hand on me, I'm going to set it off by remote control. I'll blow this crypt to—"

"*You wouldn't dare.*"

"Wouldn't I? Don't try me."

"We'll blast as soon as you poke your head out."

"All right. Go ahead, blast. But I'm one of the Children, and you know we don't die fast, if at all. I'll be able to set this baby atomic off first."

He didn't wait for an answer, climbing the steps slowly, one at a time. He reached the top step, and no one fired. He could see them now in the dim light, a dozen men, all with their blasters trained on him.

The leader demanded: "How do we know you set that thing like you say?"

"You don't."

"Well, I think maybe we ought to take you—"

John Hastings shrugged, reached into a pocket of his jumper and kept his hand there. "All I have to do is press the button," he said.

He began walking.

They followed him, at a distance. He heard their feet clacking on the hard surface, almost felt their eyes boring into his back. And the blasters. If even one of them became trigger-happy, his ruse wouldn't be worth a damn. And once they started firing he wouldn't have a chance, for the barren sphere offered utterly no protection.

He walked. The asteroid was only half a mile in diameter, and he could see his ship on the ridiculously near horizon. He saw the other ship too, a much larger one, a big, bloated, snub-nosed police cruiser.

He walked.

He reached his ship, heard a voice yelling behind him:

"Shoot! Go on, kill the dirty liar! I just went down there, and he didn't plant a thing. Kill him before he gets inside that ship—"

He was all thumbs working on the air lock lever and the blasters were firing, ripping into the hull and turning it cherry-red where they struck. They'd have the range in a moment—

He stormed inside, slammed the lock shut behind him. He saw them running for their own ship as he blasted off, acceleration pinning him down in his chair. He laughed wildly. Their bodies could not take acceleration the way his could, so let them chase him. He'd blast clear of the ring of ships and show them a few fancy turns that would crush them into bloody, shapeless things.

Now, as the police ship came up after him, he executed one of those turns. The Government cruiser was faster than his over-age scout ship, but it could not match the turn. He watched it streak off at a tangent, and he knew it would be a long time before they could turn and find him again. The acceleration was painful, but harmless—at least to one of the Children.

He knew he could get back to Earth, to his father, to Togoshira Suuki, the Japanese-Venusian half-breed who had taught him so much—and to the rest of his people.

But he had found nothing.

CHAPTER TWO

"HELLO, Suuki. How's the boy?"

"Johnny… You have returned so fast." Suuki was not a boy. He'd been middle-aged when, together with John Hastings, Sr., he'd reached the Black Asteroid. Now he was an old man with dry, parchment-like skin and big round eyes. "And is your news good?"

Johnny shook his head. "No. Nothing, Suuki—there was nothing there."

"Sometimes a man fails to see what was not meant to be obvious…"

"I didn't miss anything. There was nothing to miss. Only the Chalice and that machinery, and the murals on the wall. Those damned murals. How did they know what we'd look like?"

"They planted a seed on the three planets, Johnny. If you place a tree shrew on the ancient Earth, in the natural course of things a man would develop. A highly advanced biological science could do that."

"Where are they from, Suuki? Where?"

"Ahh—that we do not know… From the stars, Johnny, but there are many stars."

"And an age ago they left the crypt there so we could reach them. Some place there should be the secret of space-travel, interstellar travel. In the crypt, Suuki, only I didn't find it."

"I think you did well. Your examination was thorough, and it proves my point. There's nothing further to be found, nothing at all."

"I don't get it."

"We already have the secret of star-travel, if we could recognize it. That's all I will say, Johnny. Let me think."

"Okay. Hell, I'd better run up the street anyway and say hello to the folks. I'll bet they were worried."

"Worried? Aren't you the son of your father? What do they have to worry about? No, Johnny, they only worry about the future. We all worry about the future, since the Chalice…but I said I want to think."

Smiling, Johnny left the porch of Togoshira Suuki's neat little cottage and climbed the steep slope toward his folks' house. All the cottages were similar—neat and trim and inexpensive. Some seemed to hang precariously over high embankments, but the whole city had been engineered well, for many of the Children spent their entire lives there. Of all the inhabitants—other than wives or husbands of the new breed—Suuki alone was not of the children. Yet it was Suuki who had planned the city, and Suuki, along with John Hastings, Sr., who governed the city.

FURTHER up along the slope, Johnny saw a crew of laborers clearing away some debris. Glass sprinkled the rocky road for twenty yards, rocks and timber were strewn everywhere. Half a dozen panting men shoveled the ruined building material into waiting wheelbarrows, and one tall man, broad across the shoulders and thick through the chest, seemed to work harder than the rest.

"I'm back, Pop," Johnny said.

"Son! We didn't expect you for—how did it go?"

"Lousy."

"Nothing?"

"Nothing."

"Well, at least you returned safely, and a lot of us doubted you'd do that." John Hastings leaned for a moment on the handle of his shovel. A cool wind swept down from the higher slopes, but he was bare-chested and sweating. "They came up from the valley again last night," he said. "More of them than ever before, about a hundred. This time they had guns and a woman was wounded in the shoulder before we could drive them off."

Johnny frowned. "Why don't we fight back, Pop? I mean really fight back. Why don't we go down into the valleys and repay them in kind?"

"You figure it out. The police would love to get something on us, something big like that. The police are no exception—like everyone else, they hate us."

"Well, if the raids keep getting worse, we can't just sit here and take them."

"I don't see there's anything else we can do. The Children have to be careful, Johnny. You know that. We're too strong and we're too healthy—and, yes, we're too good-looking. If we competed, our men would be the finest athletes in the world, and even our women would hold their own with ordinary men. Our women would win all the prizes in all the beauty contests. We're never sick and we don't get tired easily and when we're injured we heal in a matter of hours. So the world is envious.

"Sometimes it backfires. Did you know that no ordinary person wants his sons to be big and strong and handsome, his daughters to be pretty? If they are, they can be mistaken for the Children, and they're liable to be stoned or beaten or worse. Johnny...Johnny...I didn't know I was starting all this twenty-five years ago. I couldn't know. I thought it would do good..."

"It's not your fault, Pop. The government thought it would do good, too. They knew only a small fraction of the population could visit the Chalice every generation, so they started by giving out intelligence tests. The most intelligent people went to the Chalice. And since the mutation bred true, that would give the race increased intelligence for the next generation. Only it didn't work."

"No, it didn't work. The less intelligent members of the race thought they were being gypped out of something they should have had. I don't know, maybe they had a point there. Government next tried the sick people, the mental and physical cripples. But healthy folk hollered bloody murder; they thought they had a right to be *more* healthy. Pressure groups came next, and a whole series of minor revolutions. But you know all that. Final result: there are one million Children of the Chalice in the Solar System, hated, hunted, feared…"

"If only they could construct more of the Chalices, pop."

Hastings laughed without mirth. "How? We don't understand the machine at all. If you give a spaceship to a bunch of Venusian aborigines and tell them to duplicate it, they won't know how. It's completely beyond them, because they haven't had the training and the scientific know-how. This is the same thing, only all humanity is your Venusian aborigine."

"Well, I still don't think the government acted wisely, banning the Chalice, yet not destroying it. It's out there in the asteroid belt, and everyone knows it. Hundreds have been killed trying to reach it every year—"

"And there'll be hundreds more. But the government's hands are tied. Don't you see, they can't destroy the Chalice. There's always the hope they'll be able to duplicate it and turn the whole race into supermen. Meanwhile, there are only a million of us, and we're hated."

"Well—"

"Forget it, Johnny. You must be tired, and your mother will want to see you. Why don't you go on to the house and I'll see you later."

Johnny nodded, climbed on up the road.

*　　*　　*

Ten thousand feet below him, in one of the fertile valleys that brushes the lowest slopes of the Sierra Nevada mountains, an angry crowed gathered. There were farmers and there were townspeople, mostly men, but with enough women and older children to keep the mob excited.

"Look up. Go ahead, look up. You can see it shining there, the city they built. High and mighty, snooting down their noses at us."

"They'll get theirs some day. They'll get it."

"Why wait for some day? Why not now, tonight? And why don't we give it to them?" The man who spoke brandished a club, and he looked like he knew how to use it.

"Yeah! Tonight—"

"Shh. Hold it. Here comes Bart Timmins; let's let him talk."

Timmins stalked arrogantly through the village square and people moved out of his way. Wrapped around his forehead was a dirty bandage, but he carried it like a badge of honor. His shoulders were massive, he had a barrel-chest, he wore knee-length walking shorts, and his legs below them were gnarled and muscular. His face might have been pleasant in a rough, rugged sort of way, except that he was prone to leer too much.

"Sure, *tonight*," he cried, mounting the steps of the Municipal Building. "If we go up in force, we can clean that city out."

"What do you mean, clean it out?"

"I mean mess it up, but good. I mean tear down some houses and maybe hurt some people and take some of their best men prisoner."

"What will we do that for, Mr. Timmins?"

"You afraid, Peters?" Timmins smiled coldly.

"No—no. But what good will it do us?"

"Here's what. If we can hold some hostages, if we can hold enough of them, we can chase the rest of 'em out of our neck of the woods. That is, if they want their friends back alive."

"That ain't legal."

"Is that so? It isn't even nice, my friend, but it will work. Sure, it's not legal, but wake up to the facts of life. Whenever we do something to the *Children*—" Timmins spat the word—"the police sort of turn their heads the other way. I say tonight, and I say we do all of that."

"You really hate them, don't you Mr. Timmins?"

"What's the matter, don't you?"

"Yeah, but with you it's different."

Timmins growled, told the man to forget it. Then he repeated. "I say tonight. We'll get them good tonight."

The crowd roared, and it was a long time before they quieted down. Then someone demanded: "How will we get there between now and tonight? It's ten thousand feet, almost straight up—"

"I've got a friend," said Timmins, "who owns an airport four, five miles from here. He has a dozen 'copters, enough room for a couple hundred of us. We'll get there, all right. We'll come down about midnight—and we'll be *above* the city." Timmins chuckled.

"Above?"

"That's what I said, above. They'll never expect that, they don't guard the upper regions. We'll have what we want before they know what hit them."

"I don't think that's such a hot idea," someone said.

It surprised Timmins. He scowled into the crowd, squinting against the strong sunlight. "Who said that?"

"I did." It was a girl. She was tall, as tall as Timmins himself, and quite beautiful. She came forward and the crowd parted for her. She mounted the stairs and stood directly in front of Timmins, hands on hips.

"And who the hell are you?"

"I'm a stranger, Mr. Timmins. Just got here today. But I think your idea stinks."

"Can you suggest a better one."

"I'm not going to try. I think the whole business, in general, stinks."

"Is that so?" Timmins glared ominously.

"Yes."

THERE WAS a silence. Someone in the crowd coughed and someone else tittered when the girl leered right back at Timmins and did not come off second best. Finally, he said. "What's a pretty girl like you doing traveling by yourself?"

"Nothing. Just traveling."

"Yes? Well, you're pretty enough to be one of the—"

"I never said I wasn't."

Stirring in the crowd, nervous, angry. And Timmins: "Are you?"

"Why don't you figure that out for yourself?"

"Listen, Miss—uh—"

"Bentley. Susan Bentley."

"Okay, Miss Bentley. Okay, Susie. Stop beating around the bush like that, Susie. Are you one of them?"

"I could be, at that, couldn't I? Tell me, Mr. Timmins, do you think I'm pretty enough?"

"Hell, yes. Only you're still hedging."

"I told you to find out for yourself."

"How do you suggest I do that? There's no identifying mark on the Children, although I think there ought to be one. I knew a pretty girl around here who once got beat up good because someone figured she was one of the Children. Turned out she wasn't, but we didn't learn till later."

"There's a way you can find out."

"How?"

"Hit me."

"Huh?"

"I said, hit me. Go ahead, are you afraid? The Children are strong, you know that. One of their men could take care of five or six like you, and even one of their women should be more than a match for you."

"I don't hit ladies."

"You're afraid."

"Listen—"

"You're afraid. If you hit me, and if I hit you back, harder, you wouldn't be such a big hero in front of all these people. Go ahead, hit me."

"Beat it! Scram before I change my mind."

"You're afraid." *Careful, Susan,* the girl thought. *Don't goad him too far, or he's liable to do just that. You're always ornery, and you always have a chip on your shoulder. You shouldn't have come up here and talked like this in the first place, but now that you have, you'd better convince them you're not one of the Children. Or else you'll never be able to warn those people in the city…*

Someone in the crowd snickered. Clearly, the girl was making a fool of Timmins. It never took him long to lose his temper, and now he swung his open palm and struck her across the face.

She stumbled and fell and when she got to her feet again, she was sniffling. "You—hit—me!" she wailed. "You hit me? I'm not one of them, I was only joking…"

She stood there, sniffling.

"Christ, lady, I'm sorry. It's a fool joke for you to pull; how was I to know?"

"Well, I was just joking. I even thought your idea was a good one, but you hit me."

"Christ, lady." Timmins patted her shoulder awkwardly. It failed to stop her sniffling, and everyone was laughing.

"Did you really like my idea?"

"Y-yes. Yes, I did…"

"Well, if you stop crying, and if you promise not to get in the way, we'll take you up to the mountains with us."

"Really?" She stopped her sniffling, stared at him wide-eyed.

"Sure. Sure, lady."

"Oh, thank you, Mr. Timmins." No one was close enough to see that that Timmin's hand had cut the girl's lip badly. No one was close enough to see that, nor to see that the bleeding had stopped almost at once and that now the cut could not even be seen.

*　　*　　*

After coffee, John Hastings leaned back and tamped tobacco into his pipe, lighting it and blowing blue clouds of smoke up at the ceiling. He looked at his son and he saw himself, twenty-five years before. His wife, Ellen, must have seen that, too, for she looked at both of them and smiled.

Togoshira Suuki grinned crookedly. His long white hair was as fine as flax and he let it fall to his shoulders, Venusian Upland fashion. It was the only custom of his ancient people he affected. "We are right back where we started from, are we not?"

"Yeah," Johnny admitted. "I guess so."

Ellen shook her head. Even now, nearing her fiftieth birthday, she was a beautiful woman. Her hair was graying and there were little wrinkles around her eyes and her lips, but still her face was noble enough to belong to one of the Children, although she was a perfectly normal human woman and she had never been within the Chalice. "No, we've learned something. We've learned there's nothing else to be found."

"A lot of good that does us," Johnny told her.

But Suuki grinned again. "Do not be too certain of that. Your mother seems to agree with what I said before—there may be more in what we already know than meets the eye. I am beginning to understand something... Tell me, Johnny, how did you get away from the police?"

"Why, I told them I had a baby atomic, and—"

"I don't mean that. I mean afterwards."

"I got into my ship and blasted off. I'm one of the Children, so I can take acceleration they can't get near."

"Precisely."

"Precisely?" This was the elder John Hastings. "I don't see what you're driving at, Suuki."

"Nor am I sure that I do. But one of the Children can take a great deal of acceleration. Is that correct?"

"Certainly."

"And we want to go to the stars, is that correct?"

"You're damned right it is," Johnny cried eagerly. "If we can do that, if we can get out of the solar system and reach the stars, maybe we'll be able to find the earlier race of humans who planted the Chalice here. And planted us, too. If they still exist, they've been living with the Chalice a long time, so maybe they'll know what to do about our trouble. *If* we could get to the stars."

"But we can't."

"No, we can't."

"Why not?" Suuki demanded.

"Oh, we can construct an inter-stellar drive, all right. We already have it in theory, because Einstein's light-speed maximum doesn't apply when you're dealing with subspace. But that's not the answer. No human being could survive the acceleration necessary to reach trans-light speed and, so far, no one can construct anything to ward off that acceleration."

Suuki nodded. "That, I believe, is beyond the powers of any science. It is something which cannot be done."

"Then it's hopeless?"

"I did not say that. The answer has been staring us in the face for so long that we missed it altogether. What's the old expression about not seeing the forest for the trees? Consider: the Children cannot be injured readily. When they are, they heal almost instantly. Have you ever heard of one of the Children being injured *at all* by acceleration?"

"No," Hastings said, and Johnny nodded.

"They aren't, that's why. There's something in the regenerative powers that the Chalice gives you that renders acceleration harmless. I'm sure of it. There is pain, yes, there is great pain, but any damage that forced acceleration does to the tissues of the Children is counteracted instantly. Probably, there is constant recreation of the damaged tissue, all the way down to the atomic level."

"Do you really think..." Johnny began, and his mother: "If that's the answer..."

"It is the answer," said Suuki. "I am certain it is. We can construct a starship and the Children can withstand the acceleration. It will merely be necessary, during the brief periods of acceleration and deceleration that bring you into and take you out of sub-space, to induce slumber. That way pain will be avoided—but we can travel to the stars."

"To the stars..."

THEY WERE still talking about it, hours later, when someone pounded on their door. Johnny said he would get it, crossing to the door with long-legged strides. He opened it and saw a girl, sweating, dirty, disheveled. She might have been pretty, but under all that grime he couldn't tell.

"I'm looking for John Hastings."

"Which one? There are two, senior and junior."

"I don't care. Whoever runs this city."

"That would be my father. Hey, Pop!"

"Coming, Johnny—"

"This girl wants to see you."

"Mr. Hastings?" And, when he nodded, it all came out in one gushing torrent: "I was down in the village and a mob decided to attack you up here, only they're going to do it from above you and not below, so I went with them and broke away quick to warn you before they strike."

"Huh? What are you talking about, young lady? Attack from above instead of below? Who? What for? You mean one of those mobs of rioters? We meet up with that all the time."

"More than that, Mr. Hastings. It's big this time and they came up in 'copters, and they plan on taking some of you hostages so they can tell the rest to clear out of their part of the country."

"Who are you, young lady? This all sounds so wild and incredible, an organized attack like that—"

"Please! You haven't time. Do you have soldiers?"

"Of course. But they're guarding the passes leading up from below."

"Turn them around, then. The men of the valley will be attacking above your city."

"How do we know this isn't a trick?" John Hastings had a point there, his son knew. The villagers had attempted every type of subterfuge in the past. They might—they just might—stoop this low, sending a girl with a message that would leave the passes unguarded.

Wordless, the girl reached into her pocket, withdrew a knife. She pressed the button, watched the blade snap out. Without pausing, she ran the knife across her forearm, wincing as she did so. A trickle of blood started from the cut then stopped flowing at once. The cut became a thin white line, which even as they looked, disappeared.

"I'm one of the Children," she said. "Susan Bentley. Maybe you knew my father—"

"Mark Bentley? Sure I knew him, years ago. She's legitimate, Johnny."

"Then what are we waiting for?" Johnny was already running outside, calling back over his shoulder: "Get the guard posts on the phone. Bring them around to the upper slopes. I'm taking a run down there to see that they move fast."

Then he was charging quickly down the hill, without waiting for an answer. In five minutes he reached the first guard post, not much more than an oversized lean-to set into a niche in the rock, half-hidden by the scrubby trees, that clung to the face of the mountain hundreds of feet above the timber line.

"Did you get the call?"

"Sure did. On our way up now—"

And Johnny continued running down the hill.

BY THE time he reached the fourth and final guard post, he heard the distant sounds of fighting up the slope behind him, the thud-thud-thud of pounding feet, the shout of men in battle, the sibilant hissing of blasters, the occasional flat, cracking sound of an ancient explosive rifle. Two guards were climbing out of their lean-to at the final post, and one of them nodded curtly but eloquently up the slope. "They mean business this time," he said.

Briefly, Johnny was aware that they followed him up the hill, and then he was pounding back the way he had come. As he ran, he saw the lights winking off in the trim little cottages on either side of him. Women and children would be huddling fearfully within their homes, but the men-folk were trotting up the hill in twos and threes, armed for the most part only with crude clubs. None of them spoke; talk was superfluous. Grimly, they climbed the hill.

Johnny unsheathed his blaster as he rounded the last bend in the steep path. He could see dense clouds of smoke rising under the light of the full moon. Three houses in a row had been fired, and the flames darted and licked angrily, fanned by the mountain wind.

One of the houses was his own!

The fighting centered about it, too. The defenders seemed a pitifully thin line, and they were being forced back, too. Physically, man for man, the Children certainly had the edge, and they were not outnumbered. But none of the Children could receive permits for any weapons more potent than explosive rifles. Only a few, like Johnny, used unlicensed blasters. And the result was a tremendous deficit in firepower.

The thin line of defenders crept back toward the three burning houses. There the line held for a moment, while blasting beams seared air all around them and sought them out. Then the line broke. It was inevitable, for the line could not retreat in an orderly fashion, not through the flaming ruins of the three cottages. Instead, the line broke and curled around the flames rapidly. By the time they reached the other side, they were running in confusion, and only an occasional quick volley of rifle fire answered back the steady hissing of the blasters.

Johnny plunged ahead, tried to fill the breech with his own weapon. Heat from the cottage—his own burning home—was intense, but he crouched down a dozen yards behind the stone chimney and fired blindly ahead of him. Once he heard someone scream, and he did not like the sound of a man dying in agony. Still the invaders had come to destroy their homes here in the mountain city...

In the harsh light of the flames, Johnny saw some of the invaders snaking around the cottage and plunging down the hill to left and right of him. He fired once, and then his blaster jammed and he crouched there with it, helplessly. They streamed down the hill on both sides of him, they struck with clubs and threw stones and he could hear glass shattering and women screaming. Sobbing, Johnny stood up, silhouetted briefly against the flames. He drew fire, three beams—which soared harmlessly over his head—and then he plunged into one group of the invaders.

He met them with flailing fists, sent four of them reeling with his first onslaught. Oddly, he noted that they no longer made their way down the hill. Instead, the two lines had turned back and in toward the burning houses and now swept up to the very crest of the hill. In his blind fury, Johnny did not realize they could have blasted him down with consummate ease; nor did he have time to ponder why they withdrew.

When the reason did occur to him, it was too late. They ringed him in completely, with his back to the raging flames—and only then did someone fire at him. The blaster caught him squarely in the chest and he tottered for a moment before tumbling forward on his face. He was conscious long enough after that to realize that the beam had been of full intensity and would have destroyed an ordinary man.

But he was one of the Children, and he would survive. In hours, the mechanisms of regeneration within every cell of his body would begin to function and, before the sun rose, he would be good as new. Except that they were taking him with them...

Ten minutes later, the 'copters rose smoothly from their perches further up the mountain. They winged silently into the valley below.

CHAPTER THREE

"WE'LL BUILD again," John Hastings said wearily, running a hand through his graying hair.

"We'll always build again," someone told him.

"What can we do? Do you think I like it? Do you...they have my son. They have Johnny..."

Susan Bentley tapped his arm, and when he turned around she said: "It's my fault."

"What do you mean, it's your fault? Don't blame yourself, child. If you hadn't warned us there's no telling what would have happened. And afterwards you fought like a man—"

"I have always had to fight like a man. But it's my fault. I should have broken away to warn you sooner, but I couldn't."

"Then it's not your fault."

"I knew their raid was aimed at taking a hostage. Someone important. One of them must have recognized Johnny. They've been up here before, haven't they?"

"Of course. And Johnny would venture every now and then down into the valley, anyway. A lot of the Children are bitter, but Johnny's not. He even tried to make friends down in the valley, and there was a girl once—"

"What happened?"

"I'm not sure. He never spoke much about it. He dated her a few times, and a man named Timmins, I think, didn't like it. She was Timmins' girlfriend and Johnny took her away from him. They had Johnny in jail on a trumped-up charge for six months. He wouldn't look at the girl after that, but she wouldn't look at this Timmins."

"Oh."

"Oh, nothing. It still didn't make him bitter. But that's not the point. They can't keep Johnny like that, it's not legal. Anyway, what's their purpose?"

"They're going to issue an ultimatum. If you want your son back alive, you're going to have to leave this city."

"Why me?"

"No, not just you. You don't understand, Mr. Hastings. If you want to see Johnny again, the whole city will have to be evacuated. Permanently."

"What? That's fantastic. I know they don't like us, but what have they got against our city?"

"They're just envious, that's all. They hate us. They always have and they always will. Only now they have a weapon on their side."

"It isn't legal, Susan. They can't kidnap Johnny and—"

"Your son is how old—twenty-three—well, the government will hardly look on that as kidnapping. First, because even the government doesn't hold any love for the Children, and second because they'll probably shift the blame for the fight on your people."

"All right. We've got to get him back."

"How? By raiding the valley? Then you'll really be in hot water."

"Umm-mm. Well, I'll see the sheriff down in the valley. He isn't a part of it—"

"No, but if he's anything like the law-officers on Mars, he'll shut his eyes every time."

"Well, I've got to try."

"Good luck," Susan said. "You'll need it."

THE SHERIFF lived in a small ranch house at the east end of the valley. He was a tall man and stout. He had a half-smoked cigar clamped between his yellowed teeth, and it looked like it might have been there for days.

"You're a stranger, ain't yuh?" he grunted.

"Yes."

"Where from?"

Hastings pointed up toward the distant mountains.

"One of the Children?"

"Yes."

Another grunt. "Wacha want?"

"My son. There was a raid on our city, and they kidnapped my son, name of John Hastings, same as mine."

"Don't know about that."

"Do you know about the raid?"

The sheriff yawned hugely. "There's always talk Mister. I don't know nothing."

"Weren't there some injured men in the valley today?"

"Sure. Always are. Tough breed, all the time fighting. So what?"

"We injured them. They were up in the mountains—"

"Oh, then you admit it? You attacked the villagers, eh? I didn't get no complaints, mind you, Mister, I didn't get none. But if I do, I'll know where to go, because you admitted it."

Hastings shrugged. "If there was a raid, would you know who'd be in charge?"

"Beats me. The whole thing, I mean. I don't know of any raid, Mister. Maybe you better go climb your mountain and stay put up there."

"Thanks," John Hastings said. "You've been a great help."

The sheriff lit his cigar. "Don't mention it."

Timmins strutted about the room like a rooster. "We got 'em now, men! Oh, we got 'em good. They'll have to clear out if they know what's good for them."

"I hope so," a little man chuckled. "That'll be just fine. Say, did anyone see about that young feller?" He shook his head sadly. "Hurt bad."

"Him?" Timmins laughed. "Hurt bad? I guess you don't know the Children too well. Nothing like that can hurt 'em for long. They heal, Marty. They heal quick. They're inhuman, that's what. Well, okay, let's go take a look."

Timmins strode off into a hallway, reached a door, opened it. The man named Marty gasped. "He's sitting up…"

"Sure he is. How do you feel, Hastings?"

"I'm fine," Johnny said.

"We shot him clear through the chest…" This was Marty.

"Sure," Timmins leered. "Only he healed. They always healed, every time I saw it happen. What's left of your wound, Hastings?"

"I don't know," Johnny told him. "A little white scar, I guess. I haven't looked."

Johnny smiled when the man named Marty unbuttoned his shirt and peered at his chest. "Christ, yeah," he said. "Just a little white scar."

"See?" Timmins was laughing. Something about it struck him very funny, and he didn't stop laughing for a long time.

Abruptly, Johnny stood up. "I remember you, Timmins. We had a little trouble once—but that's not why you've taken me. What do you want me for?"

"You'll find out. We're going to bargain with your people. If they leave that city of theirs, we'll let you go. If they don't, in a certain amount of time—well, you figure it out."

"Do you think they'll sacrifice their whole city, just for me? Where would they go?"

"That isn't my problem. And to answer your first question, they better."

"You're insane." Johnny took a quick step toward the thick-chested man, but Timmins pulled out a blaster and motioned him back. "Take it easy. You're liable to be here a long time, and we don't want to keep shooting you up and watching you heal again."

"IT CAME," John Hastings said. Ellen peered over her husband's shoulder, and Susan was there too. Togoshira Suuki sat off at the far end of the room—the living room of his own cottage, where the Hastings had come to live since the burning.

Hastings read: "As you know, we have John Hastings, Jr., a prisoner. If you agree to evacuate your city, permanently, we won't harm him. If you don't, we can't be responsible. You have two weeks to decide, and we want your answer not in words, but in action."

It wasn't signed.

"Could you go to the police with that?" Ellen demanded. "It proves they took Johnny—"

Hastings frowned. "They're too smart for that. It doesn't prove a thing. There's no signature, it's just a plain piece of paper and an ordinary typewriter. We could have forged the whole thing."

"Anyway," said Susan, "the law won't help. You found that out when you visited the sheriff, didn't you Mr. Hastings?"

"Yes. I did, but that leaves us with nothing."

Suuki stretched his small, thin body. "There are always means to an end, John. The trouble now is that you have been considering nothing but this problem ever since it happened, and you've lost all perspective."

"Hell, maybe you have something there," Hastings admitted, smiling in spite of himself. "Still, Johnny's my boy—"

"And we all want to get him back. The first thing you must concede, however, is that your son can take care of himself. It is not quite so urgent as you indicate. Now let's forget it completely, at least for a few minutes. I have something important to tell you, John."

"Go ahead." But, clearly, Hastings wasn't very interested.

"Johnny's visit to the Black Asteroid was the final proof I needed. There is nothing necessary for interstellar travel beyond the Children themselves. Theoretically, we should be able to take a spaceship from space to sub-space, and although the acceleration would kill an ordinary man, it would not harm one of the children, provided he had been put into a deep, hypnotic sleep. We still have your old ship up on the higher slopes, John. I should like your permission to convert it to the first interstellar spaceship."

Hastings almost jumped from his chair. "Why didn't you tell me? Of course you have my permission. Star-travel—that's what we've wanted all along. If we could find the race of pre-humans who put that Chalice out there, and—"

"There's still Johnny," Ellen reminded him.

"Yes," Hastings sobered quickly. "Well, I could take this above the sheriff's head and go to higher authorities."

Susan shook her head. "It wouldn't do any good."

And Suuki: "The young lady is right."

"Okay. Then we can mass ourselves in force and attack the valley. We can pay them back in kind and see what happens—"

"No." Suuki was quite firm. "If you did that and didn't find Johnny, they would kill him. Further, the law would then have an excuse to sanction what those of the valleys desire…"

"I think I have an idea," Susan said. "Look: when I went up by 'copter with the people of the valley, they didn't know I was one of the Children. They still don't. They had casualties up here, we buried three of their dead. I sneaked away and warned you in the darkness, but they didn't know that. Instead, they probably think it was four dead, not three. Okay so far?"

"You bet. Let's hear more."

"Well, there isn't much. I can go down into the valley and see if I can find Johnny that's all. They won't suspect me, they will suspect anyone else. I'll leave in the morning."

"We can't ask you to do something like that. There'd be danger, and Johnny isn't your responsibility. No—"

"That's ridiculous. He's one of the Children, so am I. If we don't help each other…"

Susan stood there, hands on hips. She didn't look like she'd take no for an answer.

Suuki grinned. "Let her go, John. I think she can help."

Ellen came to Susan, took her hand and squeezed it. "I don't want anything to happen to you," she said. "But if you can help Johnny—"

"I can help him, Mrs. Hastings. I *want* to help him."

And Suuki chuckled, "Maybe by the time Johnny comes back, I'll have that interstellar ship ready. It's a long way to the stars, John, but we can make it."

FIVE THOUSAND feet below *Paseo Diablo*—the Walk of the Devil—lay the town that received its name from the pass high above it. And now Susan Bentley walked boldly down Paseo Diablo's main street, looking for a familiar face. She was tired and her clothes were in tatters, for although the Children had seen her down as far as the mountain pass, she had gone on from there alone and on foot. She looked the part of a wanderer now, she looked as if she had been lost and had struggled down the steep slopes to the valley.

No one stared at her twice in the bright sunshine. Her beauty would have set her apart, but the dirt and the grime covered it, and her identity as one of the Children was, at least for the moment, perfectly concealed.

Bart Timmins saw her before she saw him. Coming out of the general store with a sack of supplies, he squinted down the street and started running. "Susie!" he cried. "You're Susan Bentley."

Susan smiled weakly. "Hello, Mr. Timmins. I—I never thought I'd make it down to the valley."

"*You* didn't think so? *We* thought you were dead. And I held myself personally responsible. I never should have allowed a delicate thing like you to go up into the hills with us."

"It doesn't matter."

"Umm-mm, yes. You're safe now."

"You see, I got lost in all that fighting, and next thing I knew, I was stuck in—in that city. It was dark and I sneaked out along one of the streets until I came to a mountain trail. I started down, but I guess it took longer than I thought. I—haven't eaten—"

And Susan began to slump forward. In truth, she felt fine. She'd had a hearty meal before leaving the city, and her amazing powers of regeneration had compensated for the wearying trek down the face of the mountain. But she'd never let Bart Timmins know that. She raised a hand halfway to her head, moaned a little, and slumped forward.

Timmins reached her in two quick strides and got his hands under her arms as she fell. He lifted her easily and, cradling her in his arms, walked toward his house, two streets away. Walking thus, he looked down at her. A lovely girl, more beautiful than any in Paseo Diablo, beautiful enough to be one of the Children. But that was ridiculous and he knew it: one of the Children did not faint from overexertion.

The girl had short-cropped, curly auburn hair. Her skin was clear and white and, despite her exhaustion, he saw a rosy glow in her cheeks. Her lips were sensuous and appealing without lip rouge; Timmons suddenly found himself thinking it would be very nice indeed to kiss her. Well, that could come later. He was pleased too with the up-tilted swell of her breasts under the thin, tattered jumper, and the feel of her legs, cradled over his left arm as he carried her, was pleasant.

Once he leaned down to brush his lips experimentally across her face, but at that moment she stirred restlessly, squirmed, sighed, and half-opened her eyes.

"You take it easy, kid," Timmins said, breathing hard. "Bart will take care of you."

HE CARRIED her that way to his house and, inside, deposited her on a sofa. Returning from the bathroom, he bathed her face with a cold wet cloth and presently she was sitting up.

"Where am I?" she said, smiling vaguely. *That pig, if he tries to touch me again. I only hope I can hold my temper...*

"Don't you worry, honey. I brought you home, and first thing I'm going to do is give you some good food. I'll bet you need it."

"I'll say," Susan told him, flashing a smile. "I don't know what I would have done if you hadn't found me."

"Well, I did, so stop your worrying."

"Did you carry me all the way?"

"Sure."

"My, you must be *strong.*"

"Well, shucks—"

"Yes, you must. Whenever there's something to be done in this town, I'd bet you take it over."

"Well, not everything, Susie. But then, if a man's born a leader, then he's a leader, I always say."

"Like that time we went up the mountain, is that what you mean? You were the leader then. Oh, I'm sure you did a good job."

"Well, we accomplished what we set out for."

"Me, I never did find out what that was. I had to get lost. I hope I didn't get in the way up there or anything."

"Naw! Not at all Susie. And I'm sure glad you're safe."

"That plan you mentioned when I came into Paseo Diablo for the first time, were you able to carry it out? My guess is you were: if you start out to do something, Mr. Timmins, then you do it. That's the kind of man you are."

"As a matter of fact, we *were* successful, honey. We got our hostage, and everything's going according to plan."

"Really? What does he look like? He must be horrible, one of those Children."

"It's all according to what you think—say, I can show him to you if you want." Timmins' craggy features were screwed into a little-boy grin. "Do you want to see my hostage, Susie?"

"Oh—I'd be afraid. Unless, unless—"

"What? Go ahead, say it."

"Unless I was sure you could protect me."

"Sure, Susie. I can protect you. I'll be right there. Want to take a look-see?"

Susan stood up, stretched, smoothed out her tattered jumper. She weaved groggily, leaned against Timmins' broad chest and cuddled there for a moment. "That feels good," she said, "because you're so strong."

He stroked her hair, said: "You must be tired. Maybe you'd like to rest first."

"No. No thanks. I am interested, and as long as you're there with me—"

Beaming, Bart Timmins led her from the room and down the flight of steps to the basement.

*　　*　　*

Johnny had studied his cell until he knew every inch of it by heart. Ten feet long, twelve feet wide, a window high up on one wall, out of his reach. A door locked from the outside. Cement floor and cement walls, a cot, a chair, a wash-stall. Quite an effective prison, without any possibility of escape.

He wondered if the Children had received Timmins' message. It didn't really matter, he told himself over and over again—no matter what happened to him, they would not give up their city. They couldn't, for then they'd have no place else to live. He only hoped they wouldn't try anything foolish. Even a small-scale raid on Paseo Diablo by the Children would be a valid excuse for the law to step in, and then there'd be no telling what might happen...

Suddenly, so suddenly that it startled him, Johnny heard a key grating in the lock. An instant later, the door swung in, and as he stood up to face it Johnny saw Bart Timmins, a blaster in his hands. But behind him was the girl who had warned them—what was her name? Susan Bentley. Then had she, after all, been a Judas? But no, that didn't make sense, and now he could see her cautioning him to silence from behind Timmins' shoulder. Probably she did not want him to show any recognition. Well, until he found out what was happening, he'd play the game her way.

"Visitor for you," Timmins leered. "Just sit right where you are, Hastings. I don't want you to scare her, see?"

"Okay, I'm not moving."

"She almost got killed in your lousy city, Hastings. Got lost up in the mountains, had to find her way down all by herself."

"He doesn't look so terrible," Susan said. "Can I go closer and look?"

Timmins shrugged. "Okay, but be careful. You never know what one of them is liable to do. Heck, you won't see anything so strange, anyway—they look human, the Children do."

"Well, I want to see for myself." And moving slowly, Susan came toward Johnny. Finally, she stood not a yard away from him, facing him directly so that Timmins could not see her face.

"Careful," Timmins warned. "Careful."

Then Susan's lips were moving, and Johnny watched. At first he didn't get it, but he knew she was forming two words again and again, silently, using only her lips. Finally, it made sense.

Grab me. Grab me.

Johnny did, in one darting motion. He grasped her shoulders, spun her around, circled her neck with his arm. She began to whimper, struggling futilely against his hold.

"Damn you!" Timmins screamed. "Leave her alone."

Susan gurgled.

"I won't hurt her," Johnny said. "But I'm walking out of here with her in front of me. You won't dare shoot. You go first, Timmins. Come on, move. We'll follow you up the stairs."

Timmins made a lewd gesture. "I'm not budging. I know you, Hastings, you won't stand there and strangle the girl. Sort of an impasse, huh?"

It was, and Johnny knew it. Timmins had called his bluff, and he stood there, helplessly. An impasse for the moment, but unless Johnny could think of something, Timmins wouldn't leave it that way long.

Timmins took a step toward them, the blaster raised. "I'm coming for you, Hastings. Why don't you just leave the girl alone and sit down? I'll forget all about what you tried." Timmins took another step forward.

Backing away, Johnny pulled Susan with him. Now what?

Closer came Timmins, and Johnny found himself backed into a corner. His hold on Susan was a loose one, although he hoped it looked like he was half-strangling the girl. One way or the other, it didn't matter. Timmins would have him again in a moment. Then the girl had made a game try, he realized hopelessly, but it had come to nothing.

And then Timmins had reached them, wrapping his free arm around the girl's waist and tugging at her. She screamed, "Let me go! Someone let me go. You'll rip me in half—"

Johnny got the idea. It was meant for him. *Let her go...*

Abruptly he released her, but Timmins continued pulling. She leaped from Johnny's arms like an arrow from a bowstring, plummeting across the room. Timmins was in front of her, facing her, and stumbling backward before her hurtling form—she was screaming and clawing at him all the time, as if she were hysterical—he collided with the far wall and landed in a heap on the floor.

Susan fell on top of him, but she heard Johnny below, and wisely she got out of the way, rolling over and over. She stopped rolling and turned in time to see Johnny cuffing Timmins quite soundly. It wasn't much of a fight. Soon Johnny climbed to his feet, the blaster in his hand. "We're getting out of here," he said.

"Damn you," Timmins cried. "Escape, go ahead, escape! But leave that girl alone."

Johnny found a coil of rope off in a darkened section of the basement. With this he bound Timmins hands and foot, stuffing a handkerchief in the man's mouth for a gag. Without saying anything, he ushered Susan from the room.

And, once they were outside: "My gosh Susan, he still thinks you were on his side."

"Sure," she smiled. "I couldn't help it if when you let me go I happened to fall all over him. But let's get out of here."

"Yeah," Johnny said. "It's a long way up the mountain."

CHAPTER FOUR

"THIS IS the ship," Suuki told them proudly.

They stood shivering on the higher slopes above the Chalice City, where now, even in summer, snow and ice clung to the permanent zones of shadow between upthrust crags and pinnacles.

"I still don't see how you got away," John Hastings told his son. "It was a week ago, but no one really told me."

"I guess we didn't feel much like talking," Susan admitted.

"She fooled them, pop. You know that part. Afterwards, well, it was a long way up the mountain, and for a time it looked like we wouldn't make it, especially when we had to spend hours in hiding because a fleet of 'copters came looking for us." Johnny shook his head. "They have a lot of power down there in the valley. And I don't think we've seen the last of it."

"What do you mean?"

"I mean that Bart Timmins is going to be good and angry. I mean that he's going to yell and holler until he brings the townspeople back up into the mountains, and then there's going to be hell to pay."

Suuki chuckled. "Well, you won't be here then."

"I don't like it, Suuki. I don't like leaving all of you like this, when anything is likely to happen. I'll be gone a long time, we can't tell how long, but if I stayed I might be able to help."

"Anyone can do your work here," Suuki told him. "But what's one fighting man more or less? You'll be doing more important things."

Susan squeezed his hand impulsively. "Yes, Johnny. Think of it—you'll be the first man to leave the Solar System behind you and head out for the stars."

"Actually," Suuki continued, "it might turn out to be a hopeless quest. Whoever the first humans were who planted the seed for us here in the Solar System, now they could be anywhere. Provided they still exist. It's as sensible to assume that some place in the long passage of time they faded away—or else went so far you'll never be able to find them."

"As it is—" this was the elder John Hastings—"you'll have a mighty hard job on your hands, son. The sky is full of stars—I know it sounds foolish saying it that way—but the sky is full. We don't know which one. We have no way to find out. It could be anyone of them, or the whole thing might turn out to be the greatest wild goose chase a man ever went on; you may find nothing out there but a lot of empty space and a lot of bright stars."

"It is our hope," Suuki went on for him, "that it won't be as bad as all that. If the old race planted the seed for us here, it is logical to assume that they planted the same seed elsewhere. Theory has it that many stars—perhaps one in three—are gifted with planetary families. Very well, a good number of those might have planets suitable for human habitation. It is our hope that on some of them the seed has been planted, as it has been planted in our own Solar System. That way, you may have a trail to follow."

"The first man to leave the Solar System," Susan mused. "I envy you, Johnny. How I wish I could go along—"

SUUKI smiled at her. "Many people do. But no, child. Only one will go. It works in theory, but it may not work in fact at all, and we will try it with one first. If Johnny can accelerate to faster than light speed, if he can find what we seek, if he can come back with his report, then there will be time to think of others going. But not until then."

The elder John Hastings frowned.

"Are you trying to say it might be dangerous, Suuki? I wouldn't want Johnny blasting off like this, not if the odds are stacked against him…"

"I don't know. I simply do not know. In theory, it should not be dangerous. But one never knows how the theory fits the fact."

"Granted. But why Johnny? Why must he be the one?"

"Because I want to go, that's why. I'm your son, and you were the finder of the Chalice. It's only right that I go—"

"That's childish," Suuki said. "Nevertheless, there is a good reason, John, although it is not what Johnny says. He has recently returned from the Chalice. He has seen it firsthand within the last few weeks, and that's more than can be said for anyone else here. He must take that knowledge of the Chalice out to the stars with him. No, there is no need for debate here: I would say Johnny is the man for the job."

And so it was agreed, but after a time John Hastings grinned ruefully. "You know, I kind of pictured the first interstellar ship as a huge, sleek thing that would make the modern planetary liners look like grubby midgets. Here it's the other way around."

The ship was a hundred-footer, a twenty-five-year-old vessel, the hull of which was liberally sprinkled with vacuum-patches. It wasn't very imposing and it looked like it might be able to bumble its way along through the void perhaps as far as Mars, provided full thrust were not employed. Instead, it would try to reach the stars…

"I admit it is no beauty," declared Suuki. "But it will run better than the appearance indicates. We couldn't afford a new ship, but we could afford a new engine: she has power, John. She should be able to reach light speed in a day, and then there are arrangements for Johnny to sleep, for, with the passing of light speed, the ship should automatically shift into sub-space and then the acceleration will be tremendous. I don't think Johnny will particularly enjoy his ride, but the ship should take him where he wants to go."

John Hastings nodded. "Then it is tomorrow. Tomorrow at dawn. Well, son, you'd better get along home and have a good meal and a night's sleep. I have a hunch you'll need both."

JOHNNY stood in the airlock as the first rose-tints of dawn caressed the eastern peaks, promising a fine day. During the night they had crammed the small ship with supplies, with food, with clothing for all types of climate, with records describing man's achievements here in the Solar System, with an arsenal of weapons and ammunition—"just in case", as Suuki had explained.

"Well—" Johnny said, clearing his throat. He felt an unfamiliar thumping in his chest, a wild beating of his heart. He was on the brink of infinity and he knew it.

"Good luck," someone said, and then the whole crowd of them were roaring, "Good luck, good luck…"

Suuki took his hand and pumped it up and down vigorously, and then his mother came and kissed him soundly on the cheek. "Johnny," she said softly, "be careful." Like that, only like that, like she might have said it when he was a kid and when he was going out into the rain and did not want to wear his overshoes. But tears threatened to overflow the corners of her eyes.

His father was last. "You're going out there for the Children, Johnny. They'll be waiting and hoping and—hell, I never was any good at speeches. Find what we're looking for, son. Find it because we need it more than anyone ever needed anything." And then they were shaking hands, and John Hastings thumped his son's back and stepped away.

Still Johnny stood there in the airlock, unmoving.

"What's the matter?" Suuki demanded. "You do understand the piloting instructions I gave you—"

"It isn't anything like that. I thought Susan would be here to say goodbye, that's all."

Ellen Hastings turned to her husband, laughing. "I believe Johnny has a crush on that girl."

"Maybe. Can't say I blame him. She's brave and she's beautiful. If I were twenty years younger—"

"Oh, *you*."

"Seriously, Ellen, if she's not here, she's not. Every minute Johnny waits gives the villagers more time to get organized. If they come busting up here and spot the starship, maybe it won't take off at all."

He hadn't spoken in any whisper, and Johnny heard him.

"All right. I thought I'd wait a minute, but I'll go. Tell Susan goodbye for me. Tell her I'll bring back some souvenirs from the stars."

And the lock clanged shut behind him.

Less than five minutes later, the ship soared skyward on a fiery, incandescent pillar. Once it cleared the highest peaks, it vanished in less time than it takes a man to blink his eyes.

FASCINATED, Johnny watched the speed indicator. Acceleration gripped and held him, but it wasn't too painful. It would become intolerable, if and when the ship reached light-speed, but by then a harmless sleeping-gas would fill the cabin and put him into a deep sleep until all acceleration had ceased.

He watched the needle climb. Ten thousand miles per second, then twenty, which was as fast as a human had ever before traveled. Thirty thousand miles per second. Like a bloated white snowball, the moon slipped by off to his left. Forty thousand miles per second...

"Johnny... Johnny, it's beginning to hurt a little—"

Startled, he turned around. Susan Bentley stumbled toward him from the entrance to the pile-chamber. Acceleration tried to hold her back, but she plodded grimly forward and soon she sat down at his feet.

"Hello, Johnny."

"Susan. How on Earth—"

"Not on Earth, Johnny. In space. I'm here."

"I can see that. You crazy kid... This could be dangerous, because if Suuki's wrong we'll never live to see translight speed."

"They said it was dangerous when I went down into Paseo Diablo to rescue you. But I made it and I got you, Johnny. I wanted to come with you this time—I had to come with you."

Johnny shook his head. "Nuts to that. This is no place for a woman, Susan. So I'm going to turn this crate around and set you down at the city before it's too late." Tight-lipped, he began fingering the controls.

Quite suddenly, Susan was upon him, clawing at his hands, pulling him away from the control board. "I want to go, Johnny!"

Momentarily surprised by her onslaught, he was thrown to the floor, and Susan came down with him. She landed on top and he tried to squirm away and back to the controls, for he knew the ship neared light-speed now and once they reached it Suuki's gas would put them to sleep and there would be no turning back. But the girl held him there because she fought with acceleration on her side, pinning him to the floor with her weight. Since the ship rocketed straight up, acceleration pulled everything to the floor, and with four gravities tugging at them, Susan's hundred and ten pounds became more like half a ton.

"Get off me, you crazy fool. In a minute or two it'll be too late."

"That's what I want. Hah—try and stop me. I said I'm going with you, Johnny."

"Listen—"

"Don't argue with me. I'm going, that's all."

"Okay. Okay, I can't do anything about it now, but after we pass translight, you're going to get the spanking of—"

"Very funny. Look who's talking." Susan straddled him and her hands were planted firmly on his shoulders. Actually, that was so much theatrics and she probably knew it: she didn't have to wrestle with him, for the dead weight alone was sufficient to hold him down. A sack of grain, under four gravities, would have been equally effective. "Look who's talking," she said again. "Careful I don't do the spanking."

Rage boiled up in Johnny. "You gawky little pip-squeak—"

"Temper..." Susan was laughing.

"So you think it's funny? You think—"

And then he said no more. Something clicked loudly above them, and a sweetish odor assailed their nostrils. "That must mean we're reaching light-speed," Susan told him cheerfully. She yawned broadly. "Umm-mm. Getting sleepy."

"That's the gas."

"Very sleepy. Johnny? Johnny, I'm afraid."

And that, he knew, was just like a girl. She had hidden aboard ship, fought for her right to stay. Now, all at once, she was afraid. She craved protection because he was a man and she was a woman. Almost, it was funny. He had tried to picture what it would be like, crossing the translight barrier. Alone at the controls, with acceleration racking every fibre of his body, watching the needle climb slowly, slowly...only it didn't turn out that way at all. He lay stretched out on the floor with a girl who temporarily weighed half a ton holding him down, whimpering for his protection.

"Nuts," Johnny said in a very small voice. And then the sweet odor increased. In another moment, he was fast asleep.

SOME TIME later, he got to his feet. Susan had managed to roll over on the floor, and she was stretched out, still sleeping, a yard away. He checked her pulse, found it normal, then staggered to the controls. He was tired, infinitely tired, and that probably confirmed Suuki's theory. All the way down to the atomic level, the cells of his body had been crushed, but—again on the atomic level—they had been recreated instantly, each atom as an individual unit. Hence the Chalice loomed larger than ever before: it healed men and it maintained their health, it made women beautiful and men handsome, but it was also a round-trip ticket to the stars.

The sub-light needle strained meaninglessly at the right side of its dial, but the second speed-gauge was functioning, its needle hovering near the number eighty.

Eighty... In a sense, it was meaningless. Eighty—eighty times faster than nature's laggard light. Or—the figures swam in his head—eighty times 186,000 miles per second. That meant they hurtled through the void at a speed approaching fifteen million miles a second. In ordinary space, of course, that would have been impossible. Einstein was no dodo, Einstein knew what he was talking about. But his universal field theory was not so universal after all; he had neglected sub-space altogether. No, it wasn't impossible to surpass the speed of light short of attaining infinite mass, you merely switched, quite automatically, from space to sub-space. And there, in a universe that contained neither stars nor space as we know it, the old laws did not apply.

"I'm hungry, Johnny."

"Huh? Oh, you're awake. Me, I guess I'm hungry too, but when you're busy with something else, it takes a woman to remind you of that."

"Well, aren't you going to do something about it?"

Johnny smiled. "The hell I will. It was your idea to tag along, and now that you're here I'd like to get some use out of you."

"So?"

"So scurry on back to the galley and fix something. Come on, scat."

Susan departed.

And soon afterwards, a pleasant odor drifted into the control room. A loud metallic clanging followed it as Susan banged lustily on a pot. "Soup's on," she cried.

Although he knew his way in the ship's cramped interior, Johnny's nose led him to the galley. Susan had done wonders. From the ship's frozen stores she had whipped together a cocktail, soup, steak and all the trimmings. Johnny said nothing. He sat down and was busy eating for the next twenty minutes.

Finally he stood up, patting his stomach gratefully. "Delectable," he said.

"You really liked it? I'm glad."

"You're all right, Susan."

"Hah. I might have known. Put a good meal inside him and a man will be your friend for life. A while ago, you wanted to spank me."

"You deserved it. But I figure now that we're in this together, we might as well cooperate."

"I might as well cook, you mean. Johnny Hastings, you're nothing but a—a gourmet. And I don't mean that as a compliment. Tell you what, though. I'm willing to bury the hatchet. Shake?" And Susan stuck out her hand.

"You're willing? I like that." He ignored her hand. "Well, okay, but we'll do it my way."

"How's that?"

HE STEPPED inside the outthrust arm and pushed it down at her side. He kissed her. He'd only meant it to be a friendly little peck, and he thought they'd both get a laugh out of it, but he found himself pulling her close, letting his lips linger on her warm red ones. Then on her cheek, her throat...

"Johnny—"

"I'm sorry," he said. He pulled away, stood off at a distance regarding her. "I shouldn't have done that."

"I didn't say I minded."

"No, that's not it. Listen, kid. We're alone. God knows we're more alone than two people ever were. Maybe the odds against ever getting back are tremendous, I don't know. But we'll have to act like we expect to return, and—well, we might find ourselves doing something we'll regret later."

Susan scowled. "Not only are you a gourmet, you're—you're a Victorian too. You're the most exasperating—"

"Stop it. Don't you see? I liked that kiss? I liked it too much, that's the trouble. I would have liked—"

"Is there any law against it?"

"No. But I...Susan, I think I'm falling in love with you..." His voice trailed off lamely.

"My gosh. Don't say it like you're apologizing. Johnny, Johnny, don't you see, just because we're stuck out here doesn't mean we can't act like an ordinary man and an ordinary woman. There's no reason to cheat ourselves, especially since we may never get back."

"We can't be sure. Maybe it's the situation we're in. Maybe—we hardly know each other."

"So, all right. Will it help if I blush every night? Why don't you use your head? Why do you think I went down to Paseo Diablo like I did? Partly for an ideal, sure. I'll admit that. Only there was more, Johnny. There was you."

"We only saw each other for a few moments before that, but, well, you hear of things like that happening. And there were those days at the Chalice City, before we took this ship up."

"Stop trying to rationalize it or you'll spoil everything. Please."

"Okay. But let me think." Without waiting for an answer, he crossed to the port and looked outside. There was nothing. Utterly and completely nothing. A complete absence of anything. Just the total blackness—that and nothing more. And because everything outside was dark, perception disappeared. It was almost as if someone had painted the port black.

Soon, they fell into a routine. They ate three times during their arbitrary day period, and then they slept— Susan in the small bedroom, Johnny in the control room. He did not try to kiss her again, but at times her nearness made him giddy with desire. Often when she wasn't looking he would follow her every move with his eyes, and he might have felt better had he known she did the same thing with him.

AND THEN one day, some three weeks after they had started, they heard again the loud clicking sound and Johnny thought he even heard Suuki's gas hissing in from some unknown vent. "That means we're decelerating," Johnny explained. "We're nearing our first goal, Susan, which happens to be the star Alpha Centauri. We're about to slow down to light speed and less, and deceleration can be just as bad as acceleration." He yawned. "Hey, I'm getting sleepy."

"Will we find anything, Johnny?"

He shrugged, strapping Susan into one of the acceleration hammocks and climbing into the spare himself. "That's a good question. I wish, well, I wish we clear atmosphere over some nice Centaurian planet and find a civilization of the first humans waiting for us. I guess that's too much to ask."

"Umm-mm." Susan was drifting off to sleep.

Perhaps, Johnny thought as he eased off into slumber, they've planted humans all over the galaxy. Whoever *they* are...

Alpha Centauri was a star of about the sun's size, but it belonged to a double-star system, and the companion, Proxima Centauri, turned out to be much smaller and fainter. When Johnny awoke he found they were back in normal space again, found that it was wonderful to see the familiar speckled vault of stars outside. And he gave vent to a primitive war whoop when he saw that Alpha Centauri had a planet.

Only one, or so it seemed, here across an unthinkable gulf from the Solar System. Almost four-and-a-half light years, and still Centauri was the closest star. Johnny looked, saw Susan still slept. Chuckling, he decided to land on the planet before she awakened.

He reached it, circled it in a tight, low orbit-retrograde. That way, the planet's rotation would serve as a brake, and did. Presently Johnny was able to take the ship down through a dense white atmosphere, which hid the surface features entirely. They came out of the billowing cloud masses abruptly, and Johnny could hardly suppress a moan. Flat gray rock stretched off to the horizon in all directions, broken only occasionally by bleak, jagged peaks, which rose almost straight up and were lost in the lowest layer of clouds. Nothing moved, and there was no green that might indicate plant-life. Wearily, Johnny set the ship down with a slight bump, sufficient to awaken Susan.

"Good morning." She stretched languidly.

"Shh! I'm testing."

"What for?"

"Everything. Gravity, density of atmosphere, gasses present. Temperature. Stuff like that. Be finished in a minute."

He was, too. But all he did after that was scratch his head.

"What's the matter."

"I don't understand it. Gravity is within three percent of Earth-normal. Density of atmosphere, the same. There's a little over twenty-two percent oxygen in the air, which is close enough. For the rest, nitrogen, a little krypton and xenon. There's water vapor, too, but very little carbon dioxide. The temperature's fine, seventy degrees Fahrenheit. I don't understand."

"What? You mean the coincidence, this planet being so like Earth?"

"I don't mean that at all."

"Well, I think it's good. It means we'll find the life we're seeking and—what? You don't mean that? Then what do you mean?"

"I mean that there's no life. Take a look."

She did, and it made her shudder. "I've never seen anything so—so dead-looking."

"Well, we might as well put some life into it, kid. Let's hop outside and stretch our legs, anyway."

THEY did, and found that there was no wind. The air had a strange, flat smell, but it certainly was breathable. After a few moments, it even began to rain, in big, splattering drops.

"Everything for life is here," Johnny said. "Except life."

"What's so strange about that? If you're religious, you say God created the world, and life on it. Well, from that point of view He's not going to create life just allover. Or, if you're not religious, you say that a happy combination of accidents is necessary to get life started. I once read someplace that the odds against those accidents all happening together—even if the climate and everything else is right, like this—are tremendous."

Johnny nodded. "I guess you have something there. Whatever the vital spark was, it missed out here. Maybe some day it will come. Maybe—hey... Maybe we're bringing it. There's bacteria all over us, there always is. If some of them stay here after we leave, and if they can survive by eating one another and then multiply too— maybe we started something. And that could be the answer to what happened on Earth, a billion years ago. If some explorer from the stars came down and left some bacteria behind him as he inevitably would, well, there's your early Earth-life. That's how it began."

Susan started to say something, but Johnny interrupted her: "Wait, I'm not finished. Remember I told you I wanted to think about something?"

"Yes. I remember." She looked glum.

"Well, I thought about it and, hell, this is as good a place for it as any. Maybe it will bring some life to this barren slab of a planet."

"For what? What will?"

"A marriage ceremony."

"What? Oh Johnny, Johnny—"

He took her in his arms and held her that way a long time, stroking her hair and kissing her. "I love you, kid. I—I want you to marry me."

"Marry you? How can we do that? You said something about a ceremony..."

"Sure did. It's going to be perfectly legal."

"I love you too, Johnny Hastings, but you're crazy."

"Think so? We won't have any witnesses, but we'll have everything else. You know what this place needs, Susan? It needs a politician—something—I know, a mayor. And there's a electorate of two, you and me. I nominate Johnny Hastings."

Susan was giggling. "I—I think I understand. You're goofy. But all right, I second the motion."

"Let's vote. My vote is for Hastings. Good man."

"So is mine." Susan was still giggling.

JOHNNY cleared his throat, spoke in a deep voice. "As mayor of this this—ah, city, I have the legal right to marry people. Do you two want to be married?" And then, in a normal voice: "Sure do."

"Oh, yes. Yes, yes," said Susan.

"In that case—" Johnny's mayor's voice again—"with the power invested in me by the electorate of this city, with the—oh, hell, Susan, I forget how it goes."

"I never knew."

"Well, then we'll have to cut it short. Do you, Johnny Hastings, take this woman to be your lawful wedded wife, to have and to hold, to love, honor, and protect, through sickness and in health, till death do you part?" He cleared his throat, then said: "I do."

Another pause. "And do you, Susan Bentley, take this man to be your lawful wedded husband, to have and to hold, to love, honor, and obey, through sickness and in health, till death do you part?"

"Well," Susan laughed, "I don't like that obey part."

Johnny kissed her. "Do you?"

"Oh, yes. I do, I do—"

"With the power invested in me and harrumph and so forth, I now pronounce you—us—man and wife."

They kissed.

"Johnny?"

"What?"

"I thought it would be silly. It was a little, maybe, but I liked it like that. We had our ceremony and we're really married. No one can take that away from us. It's much better than if we had—"

"You know," Johnny cut her short, "I think this is one hell of a lousy place for a honeymoon. Why don't we get back inside the ship and start off again? Then, after we reach sub-space, we'll celebrate."

Susan grinned. "I obey, oh lord and master, just like the mayor said."

"Then come on." He took her hand and together they entered the spaceship. After blast-off, Johnny felt good. He felt wonderful, and even, very much married. But something kept gnawing at the back of his mind, and he did not like it at all. If Alpha Centauri had been any indication of what they might find, perhaps they had set out upon a wild goose chase after all. And this planet had all the ingredients in perfect proportion—except life.

They had to find *something*. The Children of the Chalice depended on them. They had to find something and return with it, before it was too late... And then the sleeping gas came, and their return to sub-space. After that, Johnny stared out for a moment at the utter blackness. They were alone, more alone than any man and woman ever had been before. Well, that was the way a honeymoon should be. Knifing at unthinkable speed through the deep void of subspace, Johnny took his new wife into his arms...

CHAPTER FIVE

THE DAYS became weeks, and the weeks sped by and were months. Earth was forgotten; almost, it was as if Earth had never been. They streaked in and out of sub-space—seeking, seeking. Time did not matter, for there was something timeless about the black, shoreless ocean of space with its myriad bright, flashing stars, its spinning, whirling, seething nebulae, its dense black clouds of cosmic dust, its occasional nova pulsing into brief glory.

Nowhere was life. They sought it on the swollen planets of blue-white giant stars, sought it again on the worlds of a triple-star system where the sky had a sun of orange and one of green and one of somber red. But the rocky barrens became legion, the harsh methane atmospheres mocked them, the frozen ice-worlds made them depart, shuddering.

Nowhere was life—until, one day, they found it. A lush green world swam in the port as they cleared sub-space and, trembling, Johnny set their frail ship down upon it. The jungle was dank and steaming with huge, fern-like trees arching overhead to form an impossible canopy five hundred feet up in the sultry air. And the air, the air was noisy with the sounds of life. Every faint stirring of wind brought those sounds, sometimes far away and sometimes close.

"Maybe," said Johnny, and "maybe…"

But there was no sentience. A young world and a wild one, the planet would not know intelligent life for another half billion years, if at all. Wearily, they climbed back into their ship and Susan said, "We have each other."

But they had a home, too, back there along the dim, distant startrails, and Johnny told her that. "And our people," he said softly. "They're waiting and hoping. Don't you see, Susan, we can't return empty-handed. Somewhere in the galaxy is what we seek, and we can only keep right on seeking until we find it."

"But there are so many stars... We could spend a lifetime, *ten* lifetimes, looking—and find nothing."

"I know it. I know that, Susan. But look: for a long time we went and we thought there was no life anywhere, except in the Solar System. Today we found life, and tomorrow. Who knows?"

"We'll stick to it, of course. I'm sorry I said that, but I guess I'm just depressed—"

"Well, let's consider it logically. Just where have we been?"

"Umm-mm. There's Centauri and Fomalhaut—"

"And Procyon and Deneb and Wolfe's Star—"

"And Antares, Sirius, Capella, Vega and Achernar. So many, Johnny. So many..."

Johnny smiled wanly. "We're still close to the Solar System, although we're a million times further than any man has ever been. There are more stars without names than those—"

"Don't, Johnny. You make it sound impossible."

"I didn't mean it that way. What I meant was this: first we'll have to look at the known stars, and that still leaves us a lot. Let's take out the star charts."

Susan brought the charts forward and spread them out on a table. "Okay," Johnny said, pointing. "We still have to go here, and here—"

Susan copied the names on a piece of scratch paper.

Names that the ancient peoples of Earth had given the stars for one reason or another. Fanciful names and romantic. But hopeless names?

"Then here's the way it is, Johnny. Before we start getting worried, we'll have to visit Arcturus and Tau Ceti—"

"Sure, and Rigel, Altair and Betelgeuse. The sky is full of stars, kid, so stop worrying. There's still Canopus, Spica, Pollux, Regulus—hell, I could go on all day."

"Don't."

"All right, pick some names you like. It's hit or miss, it's got be that way."

"Well, I like the sound of Regulus."

"Suits me," Johnny said cheerfully, starting to triangulate the position.

"And then Betelgeuse. Hah, I never knew how to pronounce that."

"Don't try. If there are natives, they'll call it something else, anyway. They'd probably call it something that means 'sun' in their own language, just like they'd call their planet something that means 'earth' or 'world' or maybe 'home—'"

"If that isn't just like you... We haven't found anything more intelligent than a crocodile yet, but you're already giving a language to some unknown intelligence."

"Regulus it is," said Johnny, "and then Betelgeuse. Incidentally, I always pronounced it like the first half of betelnut and the plural of goose, but I wouldn't bet on it. Well, here we go."

"And after those two, try Canopus."

"You bet," said Johnny. "We've got all the time in the world." He was smiling and his words were flip, but when acceleration gripped them, he didn't feel so cheerful. The sky was full of stars, all right, and he learned that more every day…

REGULUS had not even bothered giving birth to planets. It hung in space, an exile in the bleak marches of infinity, blue and hot and very much alone. They cleared sub-space long enough to find that out, long enough to see the blue orb spewing its energy out to an empty void. It was a month later. A month gone for nothing.

"Five of them," said Susan. "Five months."

Second on their list, Betelgeuse had a great family of planets, but the star itself was red, old, feeble. None of the sixteen planets could support life. All were too far from the primary, all too cold, all had seen their good years perhaps a billion years before the coming of man. Garbed in their cumbersome spacesuits, they poked around some incredibly ancient ruins on the eleventh planet. But mostly, the ruins had crumbled into dust and what was left told them nothing except that the ancient race had not been human. Everything was built on a scale too small and the air contained thick traces of ammonia gas, anyway.

Back in their ship, Johnny lit a cigarette. They had no worry about food and their air automatically renewed itself, but such luxury items as cigarettes were fast disappearing and now he nursed this one along until it was hardly more than a glowing ember. "And for now," he said, "that leaves us Canopus."

"The names are all running together, Johnny. It's hopeless—"

He went on as if she hadn't spoken. "Canopus is a very unusual star."

"Yes? Why? They're all the same. Oh, the color is different, but they're all the same because none of them have what we're looking for." Susan began to whimper, softly, but each small sob racked her body.

Johnny placed his hand on her shoulder, but she tensed away from it. He tried to kiss her, found her face averted. She was laughing and crying, holding her head in her hands and not looking at him.

"Snap out of it, Susan. Snap out of it!"

He hit her, a hard slap that left an angry red imprint on her cheek. And after that her crying became normal and she let her head fall against his chest and used his tunic to wipe away her tears.

"I'm sorry—" he said.

"No. You had to do that. It helped, Johnny. I—I guess I was almost hysterical, but we're so alone…"

"Why don't you get some sleep? We can talk about Canopus in the morning."

"No. Every hour counts. Who can say what's happening to the Children now, after half a year? What did you want to say about Canopus?"

He lit one of the scarce cigarettes and gave it to her, watching as she blew smoke gratefully at the ceiling. "Well, for one thing, it's big. It's the brightest star in this entire section of the galaxy. It's even bright from Earth, and that's six hundred and fifty light years away. Its class is four, kid, which means it's a white giant. If there are any planets potentially suitable for life, they'd have to be in the neighborhood of a billion miles or more from their sun."

"What a place to get a sunburn," Susan said, and laughed. The hysteria that had gripped her moments before was gone completely, and that was one thing Johnny had to learn about his wife: her moods knew more variations than a chameleon. And that did not mean, he also learned, that there was anything shallow about her. She simply had many facets, and each one, like the facet of a good gem, had its inner depths.

AND WEEKS later: "There it is, Susan."

For a long time the girl stared from the port, stared into the inky depths of space outside. A star could be bright— it could be the brightest star in this entire sector of the galaxy, as, indeed, Canopus was—and still, space around it seemed very black and very cold.

Canopus shone brilliantly ahead of them as they surged forward on their regular space-drive. And something, a tiny spark, gleamed off to the left.

"Johnny—?"

"Yes," he cried. "Yes, it's a planet." And they swept in toward it.

But it wasn't a planet, not really. It had a diameter of one thousand miles. It was all a solid white color—not gleaming, not dull—just white. And the surface was flat, utterly devoid of physical features. Like the black asteroid that held the Chalice.

They came down for a landing, heard the atmosphere shrieking around them outside. The world was a thousand times bigger than the black asteroid, but still it was not large enough to hold an atmosphere for long—unless, like the Black Asteroid, the whole thing was artificial...

"The atmosphere is perfect," Johnny said, half an hour after they had landed. "Oh, it's not exactly like Earth's, but it's close enough so you couldn't tell the difference just by breathing it."

Susan was busy with some instruments, too, and she told him: "Ditto on the gravity. The slightest fraction stronger than Earth-norm, but not enough so we'd notice it. The temperature's a little hot, ninety degrees Fahrenheit."

"You can thank Canopus for that."

"What's the difference? We can stand it. But you've been using the bio-scanner, Johnny. Is there any—"

"Life? What do you think? This planet looks like a hunk of chalk. No, the air's clean of spores of bacteria or anything else. No life here, Susan."

"Then, then Canopus is no good either? I really thought this time we'd find something." Susan smiled wanly.

"I didn't say it was no good. I said there's no life here. Maybe it doesn't matter. I'll tell you this, kid: the place is artificial."

"Man-made?"

"I dunno. *Someone* made it. It's too round and too flat and there'd have to be a force field holding in the atmosphere and increasing the pull of gravity, too. Now, if it's artificial, someone made it for a reason. Suppose we go outside and find out why."

"Okay, but just you wait. I'm not going out into that ninety-degree oven wearing this jumper." And Susan was busy exploring in their clothing locker. "Hey," she called after a time, "there's nothing in here that a girl can wear."

Johnny laughed. "What did you expect? No one invited you along, honey."

"Oh yeah? Then you asked for it." There was a rustling, and then Susan stepped back into the cabin.

Johnny whistled. "You're going *that* way?"

"Sure. It's hot outside, and you're my husband, aren't you? Let's go."

Smiling, Johnny stripped down to his trousers, buckled a blaster around his waist, put fresh clips of ammunition in all his pockets. "You never know," he said. "We're liable to find anything, and this is just in case."

Susan began to giggle.

"What's so funny?"

"Nothing. Oh, nothing, really. It's only that—well, it's exactly like the old stories you read. You're a man, and you're going outside armed to the teeth, complete with spaceboots and leatheroid trousers. Me, I'm a woman, and I've seen a dozen magazine covers—well, maybe the women really *would* go like me."

Laughing, they joined hands and stepped into the airlock.

CHAPTER SIX

IT WAS hot, and quite dry. They felt the dryness at once, far worse than the heat. In a matter of hours, Johnny knew it would parch their skin and crack their lips. Already, his eyes had begun to smart. They maintained a pleasant level of moisture within the ship, synthesizing water from compressed hydrogen and oxygen tanks, but the dry heat that swept over them now would make the Sahara feel like a dank, sultry jungle.

"Well," Susan shrugged doubtfully, "what do we look for? I don't see anything, Johnny."

"No, but if *they* put this artificial planet here, it was for a reason. See? Look at that ground, it's artificial, all right. There's not a fault, a crack—nothing."

"Welcome to Cyberworld!"

"Susan?"

"Huh? What's Cyberworld?"

"That's what I wanted to ask you. Didn't you say—"

"I didn't say anything. But you said, 'Welcome to Cyberworld.' Though, come to think of it, it didn't sound like your voice. In fact, it didn't sound like any voice. It just made noise kind of inside my head."

"Welcome to Cyberworld. Respond, respond."

"Johnny, I'm afraid."

Something was speaking. Not aloud, but within their heads. If Susan hadn't heard it too, Johnny might have thought he was going off his rocker. But the voice, which was not a voice at all, spoke to both of them. And what had it said—respond…

"Thank you for your welcome," Johnny said aloud, feeling foolish. Susan was trembling despite the heat, and he draped his arm around her bare shoulder. He looked around them, saw nothing but the even, chalky expanse of whiteness. He began to sweat, and it wasn't the heat alone.

"Ask me questions, please." The whisper, which came within his head suddenly, was almost plaintive. "Ask me questions. Anything."

"Johnny, I heard it again..."

"Shh! All right, who are you?"

"I am no one."

Silence.

"Then *what* are you?"

"Ahh, that is better." Sibilant, metallic, eager, the voice spoke within his head. Susan's eyes were open wide and she cocked an ear as if she were listening to something. She heard it too, and that made Johnny feel better.

"That is much better, for I am a machine and hence the answer to your first question had to be a negative one. More particularly, I am a cybernetics machine."

"Where are you?" Johnny still felt foolish.

"I am here. Everywhere. I am the world under your feet. I am this planet."

"All of it?"

"Yes, all of it. I am a memory vault and a limited form of sentience, which slumbers until human presence is felt."

"Yeah?" Trust Susan to get cocky when she was afraid. "Then what triggered you off?"

"You did. The human brain emits electro magnetic wavelengths along a certain frequency. They waken me, and I answer questions."

"How do you speak in our language?" Johnny demanded. "None of our people constructed this place."

"I speak no language. I speak all languages. The medium is telepathy, and your brain does the translating. Although I know enough about you to speak your language aloud if I desired. You are of the planet Earth, of the star Sol. You are John Hastings, Jr., and the female is Susan Bentley."

"Susan Hastings," Susan wailed.

"Bentley-Hastings," the machine compromised. "It does not matter. Ask me questions."

Johnny chuckled softly. After the novelty wore off, it began to grow amusing. The machine had a one-track mind, provided machines had minds. Ask it questions...

"Why do you always say that?" Johnny wanted to know.

"Simple. I was constructed to answer questions. My memory vaults fill the interior of this globe completely, and literally, I can answer anything. Try me."

"How old are you?"

"Umm-mm, five millions of your years."

"Five million?"

"Certainly. I'm no youngster." The unheard metallic voice, which yet gave the strong suggestion of sibilancy, now sounded casual, almost friendly.

IT MADE Susan blush and attempt to cover herself self-consciously with her arms. "Do you think he—he can see me? I mean, the way I am..."

Johnny smiled, enjoying himself. "I didn't tell you to come out that way. But seriously, you can forget about it. Who said anything about a he? It's an *it.*"

"Well, I don't like it," Susan persisted. "Ask whatever you want Johnny, but then let's get out of here."

"Suits me. Who put you here—five millions years ago?"

The reply came at once, and Johnny somehow could picture the impossibly vast memory vaults beneath his feet shuffling and reshuffling through a maze of indexed information. "The first humans, naturally. It was after they had developed the powers of regeneration and after they had broken out into deep space. They stopped here first and constructed a planet. This planet. Me. This planet, which circles Canopus once in every—"

"Never mind. Why did they build you?"

"Elementary. I am here precisely because such as you might come. However, you are first. The very first in five million years. An age ago, the first humans journeyed out into space with a plan. Perhaps it was a noble plan, but that is not my province. They were the Lords of Creation and they knew it. Their plan was a dream—to spread their seed across the galaxy. This they did, and returned. Naturally, suitable planets were limited. Your Earth is one, Mars and Venus in your Solar System, others. All told, there are three hundred and seventy-five. Would you like to see some of them?"

"Would we," Johnny cried. "You bet we would."

There was a silence and then Johnny—saw. He didn't know how, but he saw. The picture came in his brain only, for when he shut his eyes he could see it quite clearly. Three-dimensional colored, vibrantly alive.

The metallic voice droned. "This is the planet Glehna of the star Spurl. You will observe that—"

But he paid the voice no attention. It wasn't necessary. The sun was orange, a deep, mellow orange. The fields were lush, but purple, not green. Men and women worked in them, big, strong men, comely women, naked but for loincloths.

"They are primitive on Glehna," said the voice. "Their machine age lies some three thousand years ahead of them, but they are a happy people. Next, you see Lulalim, of the star Li. Here the people are not so happy."

A SOMBER landscape, thrusting naked crags up at a heavy, black-laden sky. A blue sun, but far away, showing briefly through a rent in the clouds. It was cold. Johnny could almost feel the cold, and because he could see the picture in his head and not in his eyes, he saw also that Susan was shivering. Then she saw it too...

"The environment is not ideal for man," said the machine. "Man can barely scratch out an existence, and so it is entirely possible that on Lulalim men shall always be barbaric. You will notice, by the name of their planet, the softness of their language. A reaction to the harsh environment—"

The picture wavered, flickered as the voice trailed off. Another took its place. The depths of space—a crude, rocket-driven spaceship in the background, men spewing from its port, helmeted, space-suited, rockets strapped to their shoulders. With the reckless grace of practiced mayhem, they boarded another ship. Of their number, many died, but others there were who reached the second ship, blasted their way within, fought and died for some nameless cause. Johnny thought he saw a skull and crossbones emblazoned on one man's arm before the arm and the man disappeared in a flare of radioactivity.

"These are the people of Shilot," the machine purred. "A crude form of interplanetary travel is theirs, but they fight senselessly among themselves. They will never reach the stars."

Again the picture wavered, disappeared.

And there were others. After awhile, Johnny lost track of them. The civilizations pictured varied; some were hardly civilizations at all, others had developed to a remarkably high degree. But not one of them had yet reached up for the stars.

"All right," Johnny snapped. He could have watched all day, looking at the great pageant of a humanity that was spread out thinly across the incredible reaches of the galaxy. But the machine had no intention of hurrying, apparently, and Johnny couldn't merely stand there watching. "All right. But it seems peculiar. Are we of Earth the most highly advanced of all the human cultures?"

"No one told you that, John Hastings, Jr. There have been others, according to my records, although none of them have ever come here. Naturally, when they developed star-travel they also found their Chalices. One planted, in each case, in some remote part of the particular star system. Observe—"

The world he saw now was dark and dead, but it glowed. There was something unwholesome about that glow, the way it pulsed from horizon to horizon, flickering, brightly and obscuring the red sun. There were cities, or what had been cities, crumbled and fallen into ruin. Not very long ago, it seemed. Nowhere was life.

"They found the Chalice," the voice droned. "And because they could not all use it, war resulted. It was a deadly war, fought with radioactive weapons, and, as you can see, the planet is a radioactive corpse, festering forever in the void.

"Again, the same thing happened over and over." As the voice continued, the picture faded, another one taking its place almost at once. "This is Karnok, of the sun

Karnokkay. Here they are a generation behind, but the results will be identical in time."

The city thrummed with activity, a bustling, busy metropolis the size of New York. It had been a great port once, for Johnny could see the massive quays protruding out into an inlet of some nameless ocean. But the waters of that ocean glowed dully, dangerously. Radioactivity once more? Johnny couldn't tell, but not one ship plied those waters.

Something streaked in over the city from the south, a hurtling thing all silver and glass in the bright sunlight. It hovered over the city, and something else, smaller, winged down from its silvery belly. A few moments later a fiery mushroom erupted from the streets of the city, and when, after what must have been a long time, it was carried away by the winds, the city was dead...

"They fight for their Chalice. One nation has it, the other wants it. The war will engulf both in destruction."

"That couldn't happen on Earth," Susan said. But it sounded more like a question. "After all, we don't have nations. We have one world state, and it's a democratic one."

"Sure, but there are pressure groups. You saw them for yourself. And what about the way the Children are treated? Civil War could mean the same thing, but—"

Said the voice: "On this next planet, you will see—"

"That's enough. I have another question. Who are those that created you?"

"I have said, the first humans."

"Yes, I know that. But who, and where?"

Silence. Then: "That information is classified. One moment, please."

Johnny and Susan looked at each other hopelessly.

"CLASSIFIED? What does he mean by classified?"

Johnny grinned wearily. "Not he, it. But search me, kid. I don't know what it means…"

Suddenly, something groaned beneath their feet. Johnny blinked, and when he looked again, a portal had opened in the flat white rock of the planet. One moment there was nothing—the next, a circular pit awaited them.

"Enter," said the machine's voice. And, when they failed to move: "You have nothing to fear, provided your intentions toward the first humans are friendly. I have said enter. Enter."

Johnny shrugged. "What do you think, kid?"

"Don't look at me. But we're not getting anywhere by staying here, that's for sure."

"Well, okay." And Johnny stalked toward the pit.

As it turned out, a flight of stairs awaited them, and it reminded Johnny of the nine steps leading to the Black Chalice. Naturally, he thought, the same builders…

The stairs led around and down, descending in a circular fashion for about a hundred feet. And at the bottom, they found themselves in a small, square room with a soft, almost spongy floor.

"Lie down."

"Huh?"

"I said lie down. We will conduct certain psychological tests to determine the frame of reference in which you hold the first humans. If it is a friendly frame, you go from here with the information you seek. If it is hostile, you do not leave here at all. The vault will simply close in upon you. The third alternative is this: you may withdraw now and depart without receiving any information."

Susan frowned. "If we flunk whatever test he has up his sleeve, we're buried alive. All right, *it*. *Its* sleeve. But Johnny, what kind of test…"

"That beats heck out of me. How should I know? But look, we've got nothing against these first humans, have we? We came to find them in the first place."

"Yes, that's true."

"Well, don't get optimistic on me. It's not entirely true. Subconsciously, we're probably both bitter. The first humans planted the Chalice in our Solar System, so, as a result, we're hated, feared, fought with—"

"You mean maybe *it* will interpret that as hostile?"

Johnny shrugged. "A possibility. All I'm trying to say is this: we can't be sure. This machine of a planet will be completely objective, but what it calls hostility might be something we wouldn't think of that way at all. Think it's worth a try?"

"Johnny, you sound almost flip. But—"

"I know. Our lives depend on it. I don't know what the answer is, but it's a cinch we won't find what we're looking for unless the machine tells us. So, I think we ought to give it a whirl."

For answer, Susan turned and faced him, placing her arms around his neck. "I thought so all along, but I wanted to hear you say it."

"Well, I said it."

"Kiss me, stupid. Umm-mm…"

And then they had stretched out side by side, on the spongy substance, while the voice repeated again and again, "Lie down, lie down—ahh, that is good."

A pause. Then: "You are asleep." Simply stated, with no fanfare, no preambles. The ultimate in hypnotism, for Johnny felt one brief instant of vertigo, reached out to clutch Susan's hand, but didn't make it. He was sound asleep less than a second after the voice commanded it.

HE AWOKE with a headache. Dimly, he half-remembered dreaming, and while he could not remember what he dreamed, the thought of it somehow left him strangely frightened. "Susan?" he whispered. "You all right?" He smiled. There are certain places, certain happenings that make you want to whisper. This crypt with its dreaming, hypnotic sleep was such a place.

"Yeah, I guess so. I have a headache."

"Me too. Well, I guess we passed the test. At least, I see no indications that we're locked in here."

Then, came the metallic voice: "You are quite right. While your brains display a marked amount of hostility and ambivalence toward the Chalice, they regard the first humans only in reverence. As a result, the classified information is yours for the asking. Ask me questions."

"Where are the first humans?" Johnny demanded.

"They exist in a star-system that has not been named by you."

"Oh. In that case, it's probably hundreds of light years from here. A long trip, but we can make it."

"You do not understand. You have not named the particular star-system because it is remote. Truly remote. It is in the galactic satellite, which in your language is referred to as the Greater Magellanic Cloud. It is therefore—"

"What?" Johnny gasped. "Magellanic Cloud—that's so far from here that we couldn't reach it in a dozen lifetimes, even with our sub-space drive."

"To be precise, the distance is 26,000 parsecs, or 86,000 light years. Although it is actually within the outer fringes of the Milky Way Galaxy, the Greater Magellanic Cloud is, for all intents and purposes, an exterior galaxy."

Susan pouted. "That's great. Oh, that's just wonderful. Now that we know where the first humans are, we can't do a thing about it."

"Ask me questions," the machine purred in their minds.

"Can we get there?" said Johnny.

"Of course."

"That's ridiculous." Perhaps, he thought, the machine had misinterpreted the question. "How can we get there? Not with our sub-space drive?"

"That is correct. Not with your subspace-subspace-subspace-subspace…"

Quite suddenly, the machine voice, which spoke and yet did not speak, sounded like a broken record. The same syllables, over and over again.

"It broke down," Susan wailed.

"…spacesubspace…"

Johnny couldn't help smiling, in spite of the situation. "Well, after all these millions of years, I guess it kind of needs oil. But that's a hell of a note, when we're getting so close to the answer—"

"…subspacesubspace…ah! I oil myself, you see, but sometimes it takes time until the various units can attain harmony once more. Now, what were you asking?"

Johnny wiped the sweat off his forehead with a trembling hand. "How can we get to the Greater Magellanic Cloud?"

"I can send you. That, also, is why I am here. The first humans planned it this way, for beyond sub-space there is something, which for want of a better term, I call folded space."

"I don't get it," Susan protested.

"Elementary. In sub-space, you can travel far faster than light, but not fast enough when intergalactic distances must be coped with. In folded space, that is precisely what happens—space is folded. You would not understand the science behind it, but is precisely as if space were a sheet of paper and you could somehow fold it, corner to corner. Thus, to get from one corner to the other it would not be necessary to travel across the length of paper. Instead, through folding the sheet the corners are made to coincide. Travel is instantaneous. And such is folded space."

Johnny chuckled grimly. "Okay, I won't argue with you. When can you send us?"

There was a pause. Then: "Now, if you wish."

"We sure do."

"But much has happened on Tawroc since I was created..."

"Tawroc?"

"Tawroc, the home of the first humans. I think you will be sorely disappointed, for, although they created me—"

"Well, just let us decide that."

"Good enough. You will, naturally, need a command of the language of Tawroc. *So*—"

JOHNNY was aware of an unfamiliar rustling with his head, and the suggestion of pain with it. Looking at Susan, he saw her face was strained, twisted, distorted. Then, did the pain affect her more strongly? He reached out to comfort her, but abruptly, the strangeness within his head subsided, and his wife relaxed visibly.

"It is done," the machine told them. "You will speak Tawroc when you have to. But, because I do not believe you will find on Tawroc what you seek, I will await your return here. Now, are you prepared to leave?"

"Yes," said Johnny.

"No." This was Susan, indignantly. "If you think I'm going any place where there are people, dressed the way I am—"

"Undressed, you mean," Johnny laughed.

Together, they climbed the stairs, returned to their ship, got clothing for Susan and more arms for both of them. In the crypt once more, the machine's voice was impatient.

"Vain," it mused. "Humans are so vain. But I perceive you are ready. Goodbye, good luck, but I think you will be a lot wiser when we meet again."

Johnny looked around uneasily. "I don't understand," he admitted. "What can that mean, we'll be disappointed with Tawroc? The birthplace of humanity, kid—can you imagine what that means? It was there, millions of years ago that the seed was spawned. Now it's spread out over the length of the galaxy. But Tawroc, Tawroc should be as close to heaven as a man can ever get and still live."

"Eighty six thousand light years," was all that Susan said. "Can it be done…?"

Johnny did not know, nor did he have a chance to ponder it. Something seemed to grip him and twist, and he felt, impossibly, that he was being turned inside out. It failed to last long. He knew, dimly, that it could not. Even the Children would not long survive the exquisite pain that lanced through every atom of his being. He heard Susan screaming, saw her as through a dense fog, far, far away. He tried to reach her, but she floated away on that unreal sea of fog, the wraiths of it swirling and billowing between them. He called her name, heard it rebound at him from all sides, *"Susan, Susan, Susan…"*

The fog caressed him, brought with it a brief awareness of utter cold. Tumbling headlong into a pit of that cold, Johnny remembered nothing more...

CHAPTER SEVEN

THEY WERE on a beach, a wide, sandy beach that sloped down gradually until it met the sea. The water had a strangely reddish cast and Johnny thought first of plankton until he looked up and saw the sky, too, was a glowing crimson. Clouds obscured the sun, but he knew, if he could see it, the daystar would be somber red. A hundred yards down the slope, the waves shattered themselves to red-spray, billowing and roaring and tumbling back upon the waves behind them. Fury lashed those waters and it might have been a hurricane. But the air was quiet. Then the sun was close, and over on the night side of the planet, one or more big satellites must have whipped the nameless ocean to a frenzy.

"Where are we?" Susan asked, propping herself up on one elbow and brushing the sand from her hair. And, when Johnny laughed: "I know it's a stereotyped question, but where *are* we?"

"Tawroc, I guess. Wherever Tawroc is. That machine wasn't kidding."

"That's fine," Susan said. "That's just fine. He—*it*—only neglected to tell us one thing."

"What's that?"

"How the hell are we going to get back from here?"

It was a good question. Canopus and their ship lay across the length of the galaxy from them, and Canopus was a thousand times brighter than Sol. Even Canopus, at this distance, would be nothing but a tiny mote, lost in the deep, far away clouds that formed the Milky Way.

"Later," Johnny said. "Ask me that later. Right now—hold on, what's that?"

Someone was coming up the beach toward them. At this distance he wasn't much more than a tiny dot, but soon he came closer and they could see it was a man. He hailed a greeting at them and it was in some strange, alien tongue. *"Kortu!"* he cried, and again: *"Kortu!"*

"That means hello," Johnny found himself saying, and then, startled, he raised a hand to his mouth. He'd said: *"Chora ben kila tok,"* They were nonsense syllables, they could have utterly no meaning for him or for Susan. Yet, saying them, he understood.

"My gosh," said Susan. She didn't say it in English, but Johnny comprehended.

"I think I understand," he mused, again in the perfectly understandable alien tongue. "That machine wasn't fooling, he gave us the language of Tawroc, but it remained dormant in our brains until a word in the language triggered it off. Now we know it, and speak it."

They couldn't doubt this one final improbability. The machine, indeed, had seemed capable of anything, and one minor miracle more or less wouldn't matter.

By now, the man who had hailed them was approaching, and Johnny watched him trudging along through the sand. He was middle-aged, with a long, careless shock of iron-gray hair, an intelligent face and a short, stocky figure.

"Kortu," Johnny cried. "Greetings…"

"Greetings yourself. What are you two doing down here on the beach?"

"We just arrived," said Johnny.

"Fine weather we've been having, if you go in for admiring the weather. Personally, I don't. Some primitives still do, and I thought the way you were dressed, and all—"

THE MAN wore a sort of coverall, but if there were any seams, Johnny failed to see them. The outfit was of some metallic material, and it seemed to flow fluidly with every motion the man made.

"We're strangers here," Johnny told him. He was beginning to enjoy himself. He could picture the man's face when he was told that the two before him had come from the stars. A culture-dream realized, after how many millions of years?

"Strangers? I don't understand." Then, suspicion crossed the man's face. He came close to Johnny, stood on tiptoe, peered into his eyes. He relaxed. "Oh, you're blue eyes, all right. Is the woman yours?"

"Yes, my wife. We have come—"

"Haven't seen any brown eyes in days. Guess we chased them off this continent. If we keep winning the way we are, the sides will have to be changed, of course. Too bad, for I really learned to hate brown eyes."

"We have something to tell you. We—we're not of Tawroc."

"Hah-hah. Not of Tawroc. That's good. Hah-hah."

"I'm not joking."

"Well, then explain yourself. How can that be?"

"We are from the stars. Wait—don't laugh. You see the Milky Way Galaxy in the sky at night, don't you?"

"See it? It practically covers the entire sky. Of course I see it. So what?"

"So that's where we come from. A planet called Earth, circling a star called Sol. A generation ago, we found the Chalice you left, and—"

"That's interesting." The man clucked his tongue once or twice, nodded. "That's interesting. You plan to stay long? Look me up some time in Chandros City if you do. Meanwhile, guess I have to go on down the beach and look for brown eyes. Never know where they're liable to pop up, the rats."

Johnny felt something was wrong. He couldn't tell what, but it was something. Perhaps the man hadn't understood.

"My name is John Hastings," he said. "This is my wife, Susan. We're not native to Tawroc. We come from the Milky Way Galaxy, thanks to the Chalice your people planted in our Solar System, an eon ago."

The man yawned, stretched, watched the tides come booming in. "You already told me that. Have a nice trip?"

"Man, don't you realize we've come across eighty-six thousand light years to see you? You planted our seed on Earth, and we spawned. We found your Chalice—"

"You already told me that, too. And don't you think I know my history? Too bad you didn't arrive a bit earlier, you could have taken part in the brown-eyes blue-eyes war. Almost over, I think. Say, wait a minute... I thought there was something fishy here."

Wordless now, the man peered intently at Susan's face. "Ah-hah!" he cried triumphantly. "Brown eyes, I might have known." Before Johnny could stop him, he had reached into a pocket of his coverall—the pocket seemed invisible, but it was there, for when he thrust his hand laterally across his chest, it disappeared within the garment. He came up with a small, slender tube, pointed it at Susan.

Something glowed briefly and she did an abrupt flip-flop in mid-air, then fell on her face in the sand.

"SUSAN," Johnny cried. He kneeled by her still form, turned her over tenderly, felt for the heartbeat. It was there—but faint. He stood up, rage contorting his features. "Damn you—"

The man clucked softly, returned the weapon to its invisible sheath. "Are you sure *your* eyes are blue?" he demanded.

Johnny hit him, felt his knuckles crunch on the man's thin jaw, watched him fall and land on his back.

Wiping blood from his lips, he looked up at Johnny. He seemed very confused. "Why did you do that?" He shook his head sadly. "Why?"

"Damn you—"

"Oh, don't worry about your wife." The man didn't wipe his mouth any longer, for the bleeding had stopped. "She'll be up and around any minute now. Of course, she'll have to go to Casualty Island for the duration. But I have a suspicion this war won't last much longer, anyway."

Susan stirred. Her eyelids fluttered, and, in a moment, she got to her feet groggily. "What hap—"

"Don't talk," the man protested. "It's against regulations. I got you fair and square, there's no denying that. There'll be a boat leaving for Casualty Island this afternoon and, naturally, you'll be on it."

Susan frowned. "What's he talking about?"

"I don't know. I think he's crazy. He must be crazy."

"Now, listen, young woman. You've got to follow the war-ethics. There wouldn't be much sense to warfare if you didn't. Although, I must admit some people are growing bored with it, anyway. Say, maybe you'll have some suggestions. What do you do on your world for diversion?"

"Well," Susan began, "we—"

"Skip it," Johnny told her. "He's a first-class nut. Uh—Mr.—"

"Nabish, name's Nabish."

"Nabish, where's the nearest city?"

"Right back of the beach that way, two or three miles. Depends on whether you mean the metropolitan area or the city itself. I always say—"

"Thanks," Johnny told him, leading Susan away. Nabish clucked his tongue in sad confusion as they departed.

THE CITY was quite beautiful. They saw it first from a rocky highland overlooking both it and the beach. It spread out below them, circular, the avenues radiating from a central plaza like spokes from the hub of a wheel. Flat-roofed and square, all the buildings were low, graceful structures.

"Want to go down there now?" Susan asked.

Johnny nodded. He couldn't get the man named Nabish out of his thoughts. He'd seemed intelligent, even perfectly rational, if you could disregard that business about a brown-eyes-blue-eyes war. He even seemed to understand when they said they'd come from a far world, from the Milky Way Galaxy, which certainly should be the predominant feature of the night sky here. But—if he understood—he didn't care. It failed to stir him. And Johnny, for his part, had expected the people of Tawroc to receive Susan and himself as a father might receive his long-lost son. Racially, that was the relationship, but

Nabish's attitude, assuming the man was sane, could foster only confusion.

A broad avenue swept around the outer fringes of the city's radiating streets. This was the rim of the wheel, Johnny thought idly. He'd have been interested if they hadn't met Nabish first but, with Nabish gnawing at the back of his mind, architectural beauty left him cold.

The avenue was crowded with vehicles, but so fast did they streak by that Johnny could hardly see their design. Vaguely, they were tear-drop-shaped, hugging the ground and zooming over it as if they somehow did away with friction. There were pedestrians, too, waiting to cross on either side of the avenue. Every now and then, one would dart out into the street and hurtle, dodging and weaving, to the other side. There was no screeching of brakes as the vehicles sped on by, and not one of the pedestrians had an easy time of it.

"People can get killed that way," Susan said, and laughed nervously.

"Not Chalice people," Johnny reminded her. "Oh, they can be maimed, but they'll heal."

"Still, you'd think they'd develop some kind of traffic control. The accident rate must be awful high…"

Johnny whirled around then. Someone was screaming. He caught a brief glimpse of a woman darting out across the street, saw one of the zooming vehicles bear down on her. She tried to avoid it, but the vehicle bore on, swerving neither to left nor to right. There was a crunching sound, and more screaming as the woman was borne along for a score of yards under the vehicle. A moment later, her broken, bloody form remained on the highway, while more cars streaked past.

"How awful." And Susan averted her face.

A BELL clanged somewhere, and a portal opened in one of the square buildings. Out came four men, carrying a stretcher. They waited several seconds, then ran out across the road with it, scooping the woman up and carrying her back to the building. In a moment, the portal shut.

Two men stood a few feet off at Johnny's left, and he heard them talking. "Shame about Lidun," one said.

"Yes. There was to be a party at her house tonight. But it will be two days before she's herself again."

"Umm-mm. Yes. She got mashed pretty badly, so I guess they'll have to give her new features. Well, she never was very pretty."

"Her husband's going to be furious. Hah, poor Skandar. That's the third time this month his wife has met with an accident. I always said Lidun wasn't the most graceful woman in the world."

"What you forget is that Skandar is brown-eyes, and a casualty, too. He won't know anything about this till after the war is over. Lidun's suing for divorce anyway—can't blame her, not while this war is being fought."

Johnny cleared his throat. "Hello," he said, smiling.

"Eh? Hi, neighbor. Don't think I know you."

"My name's Hastings."

"An odd name. You from Syloph or one of the mountain cities?"

"No. Some place else. Does this sort of thing happen all the time?"

"What sort of thing?" The two men looked at each other queerly.

"This accident. I mean, I should think you'd have a way of regulating traffic—"

"Where *are* you from?"

"A long way off. What I mean is—"

"He must be one of those mountain yokels," the second man said. "Only thing they have to worry about there is the animals. But then, that can be pretty rough. Yes, friend, this sort of thing happens all the time. Why shouldn't it?"

"Why shouldn't it? Well..."

"It's perfectly harmless. Lidun will be dodging cars again in two days. Unless they call her number on the lottery and decide she's to be un-Chaliced."

"Don't tell me that can be done?" Johnny demanded.

"Why, naturally. Where did you say you were from?"

"I didn't."

"Well, wherever it is, you certainly must know about the lottery. It's just to keep life interesting, friend, and the Almighty knows we need something to keep life interesting, eh? One each month out of every hundred thousand people is un-Chaliced. Poor things, a lot of them commit suicide. But then, you can't blame them. Funny thing about the rest of them, they go off to live in the mountains some place—"

"No," his companion corrected him, "in the desert. They go off into the desert."

"The mountains!"

"Desert."

"Mountains."

"Des—"

The first man took one of the tubes from his coverall, pointed it at his companion, who glowed briefly, then fell. A bell clanged again, and the stretcher-bearers shuffled out of their building, retrieved the body, returned inside with it.

"As I was saying," the first man went on, "they hide off in the mountains some place, and—I'll be un-Chaliced. He was right. Jor was right. It's the desert, I remember reading something about that. Well, I'll have to apologize to Jor when he's up and about again. Anyway, what were we talking about?"

"Forget it," Johnny told him. "Listen, who's your civic leader here? I'd like to see him."

"Civic leader? What's that?"

"An official. A mayor, or president or city-planner. Something—"

"There's no such man."

"Your government, then. Where's your government building?"

"Government? Oh, a body that governs. Why, there's no such thing. Be an awful lot of waste, wouldn't it? What do we need a government for?"

"Isn't there anyone with authority?"

"Of course. Each man's his own authority. The Almighty knows life is boring enough, without someone having to restrict your behavior. Say, how come you're so naive?"

"Forget it," Johnny said again. "How about a scientist? I'd like to see a scientist."

"Well, every man to his own opinion, I always said. But what do you want to see one of those idiotic hobbyists for?"

"Hobbyist? Don't you have any professional scientists?"

"What do we need them for? We've got everything we want. But, as I've said, there are some who dabble in science. Hobbyists. Want to see one, eh? Well, umm-mm, let's see. Yes, Condan would be your man. Condan."

Here the man paused, took what looked like a sheet of paper from his invisible pocket, wrote on it. "This is Condan's address, my friend. What did you say your name was?"

"Hastings."

"Right, Hastings. See you some time, but then, if you meet with an accident between now and then, I might not recognize you. Keep interested."

CONDAN'S house was like all the rest, and Johnny paused before running his hand in front of the electric eye on the doorframe.

"I don't like this place," Susan said, shaking her head.

"I don't understand it. Well, maybe this Condan—" And he heard chimings within the place when he ran his hand across the electric eye.

In a few moments, a woman came to the door, tall, angular, unpretty. "Yes?"

"We'd like to see Condan?"

"What for?"

"Huh?"

"I work here, so I have to see the horrible old man, but why anyone else would want to see him I cannot understand."

"Still, we want to see him."

"Humph! I'll tell him he has callers."

And the woman plodded back through a foyer, muttering to herself.

Condan followed her when she returned to them a few moments later. Condan was short, bent, quite thoroughly bald, with beady little eyes that darted furtively first from Johnny to Susan and then back again. "Yes?" he demanded, his voice squeaking effortlessly over two octaves while it uttered that single word.

"You're a scientist," Johnny said. "We'd like to speak with you about—"

"Very well, young man. Whatever it is, very well. But first allow me to apologize for my hobby. Yes, I am a scientist, but not out of direct choice. I tried arson as a hobby first, but I'm too clumsy, and I burned myself up pretty badly after three tries. Assassination, next, but it's a thankless labor, for no matter how well you do your job, your victim is up and around within a few days. Next I tried…but I'm boring you, and we can't have that.

"In short, I tried everything. Science alone remained, and so I dabbled. Actually, it does have its rewards, for I have heard of someone who met with an accident while using acid, and—"

"I see," Johnny told him wearily. "What science do you specialize in?"

"Why, none in particular. All of them. I'm the word's foremost scientist, I'm sorry to say, but then, remember it wasn't out of direct choice. I just had nothing to do with my spare time, you see."

"I still don't like this place," Susan whispered.

But Johnny said: "We don't come from Tawroc."

"Umm-mm. That's nice. Perhaps I can write a paper. But sadly, few will read it. What precisely do you mean, you don't come from Tawroc?" Mild curiosity showed on Condan's features. He scratched his bald head.

"Well, do you know any legends of your ancestors, ages ago?"

"Oh, yes," Condan answered brightly. "I know of many such legends. There is, for example, one that tells of our people before they had the Chalice. It must have been terrible, because people are bored unless there are accidents, and without the Chalice accidents too often would prove fatal."

"I don't mean quite that far back," Johnny persisted. Part of his mind by now realized that their quest was a hopeless one here on Tawroc. But, doggedly, he stuck with it. "I mean soon after your people developed the Chalice."

"Oh, yes. That legend has always been one of my favorites. We went out to the stars—some say even across the great gulf of peace to the Milky Way Galaxy. And there we set the seed for mankind. It is very interesting, although, if you dwell upon it too long, it becomes boring, like everything else."

"We're from the Milky Way Galaxy," Johnny told him. "We are the fruit of that seed. And we've come a long way."

"I believe you. I do. I really do. And let me tell you that's very nice, young man. Yes, I certainly must write a paper, although I doubt if I have the funds to publish it. Well, perhaps next year."

"Darn it." Susan finally had lost her temper, and now she raged at the little scientist, who did not quite know what to make of the situation. "Darn it! You might at least congratulate us. You should all feel like a—like a God, almost. But you just stand there and say that's nice. Darn it—"

"She must be bored, poor thing," Condan decided. "Did you ever think of taking her away to the mountains for a few months? Some of the animals are quite ferocious, and it's usually a stimulating vacation. I would—my word, it's three o'clock."

INSIDE, something had clicked loudly, three times.

"I'm the lottery man this month, you know. Three o'clock. That makes you two the winners. You'll be un-Chaliced, of course. May I be the first to offer my sympathies?"

"Keep your hands off me," Susan cried. Condan had been shaking his head sadly, stroking her shoulder.

Johnny spoke, jabbing his finger against the scientist's frail chest with every word. "We're not going to be un-anythinged. We're getting out of here."

"Where will we go? I appreciate your feelings, young man. But it is now known all over the planet that two people answering to your descriptions have been selected for the lottery this month. If you resist, you'll be taken in time. But, naturally, resistance could be amusing. Have fun."

Johnny's head was swimming. He knew now that he'd expected a veritable godhood in the men of Tawroc. Instead, he'd found—this. But still, he wasn't ready to give up. He said, "Listen. We came here for help. We have a Chalice, which you planted, in our Solar System, but it breeds trouble. Few can use it, the rest are jealous. If you can let us know how to build another one, many other ones, our trouble will end, and—"

"I'm not so sure, Johnny," Susan told him. "Maybe then our troubles would just begin."

Shrugging, Johnny ignored her. "Can you do that? Can you teach us to construct another Chalice?"

"Naturally, young man." Condan nodded. "But it won't do you any good, you realize."

"Why not?"

"You're for the lottery, remember. You'll be un-Chaliced. Then, if I remember my history correctly, you won't be able to travel between the stars."

"What do you mean, history? Don't you have space travel?"

"Whatever for? It's boring enough on the surface of Tawroc, but can you imagine how bad it would be with a lot of nothing all around you. There hasn't been a spaceship built here in a hundred thousand years. Well—ah, that would be the Lottery Committee."

The door-chimes had sounded, spilling their musical notes up and down the range of two scales. Johnny heard the angular housekeeper opening the door, saw four men enter.

"Where are they?" said one.

"Here." Condan pointed.

"Well, are you two ready?"

Susan smiled wanly. "Johnny, honey? Oh, Johnny, do you mind if I cuss?"

"N-no."

She turned to the Lottery Committee. "Go to hell."

And then she was giggling. The letdown had been tremendous—for now Johnny knew that Tawroc and its first humans could offer them no help. They'd come across the length of a galaxy and beyond for nothing, and now they must go back to their people and say they had lost. But for Susan it was worse. Her high-strung nature had plunged up and down like a wayward rocket, and her rage fringed on hysteria.

"Kill them, Johnny. I don't care how, I don't care—but kill them..." And then her head was against his shoulder and she was sobbing. "Kill them, kill them...Johnny, oo-oooo..."

Johnny wanted to comfort her, knew she'd need a lot of it. But there wasn't time. Condan knew what he was talking about, and if they were un-Chaliced, there'd be no returning, ever...

On the other hand—and suddenly Johnny's heart bobbed up into his throat and remained there—the machine had never told them how they could leave Tawroc.

Had, in fact, never told them they could leave at all.

The machine was only that—a machine. A thinking machine, perhaps, but completely objective, impartial. This world of Tawroc was different. Trouble was, *it didn't care.* Its people cared about nothing. The Chalice had made their ancestors too perfect, and the result was ennui. The whole world of Tawroc, almost, had a personality, if a negative one. It didn't care. It cared about nothing but its fantastic rules and regulations, grown, monstrous through boredom.

Except for the lottery. The lottery mattered. The lottery said that Susan and Johnny must be un-Chaliced, hence exiled unwillingly on Tawroc. Johnny's head whirled hopelessly. There was no escape—nothing could be done. In his mind he called over and over again to the machine. *Help us, help us, help us...*

Unconcerned, indifferent, the four men of the Lottery Committee stalked forward. Johnny backed off into a corner, leading Susan by her hand. He wondered dimly if the machine, circling Canopus almost a hundred thousand light years away, somehow could see what was happening.

He wondered—and something seemed to chuckle within his head.

Raging, he ran forward, caught the first member of the Lottery Committee and hurled him dazed, against the wall.

He plowed into the second, his fists flailing. Shaking his head, the third man removed one of the tubes from his coverall, pointed it.

Johnny felt a moment of pain almost too brief to register on his brain. He pitched forward on his face.

Susan followed him down, fell across him. The two injured members of the Committee shook themselves, and, together with their companions, lifted their unconscious burdens and stepped out into the street with them.

Condan waved goodbye and went back to his primitive laboratory.

The Lottery Committee had to wait half an hour before they found an opportunity to cross the street.

CHAPTER EIGHT

"ARE YOU all right, Johnny? Johnny? No, don't try to sit up."

"Stop worrying. We don't break easy. But I'm a little fuzzy on the details. What happened?"

"Probably, it was the same weapon that man Nabish used on the beach, only the effects lasted longer this time. We seem to be in some kind of a—a hospital."

There were two beds, one empty now. Johnny lay on the other, Susan bending over him anxiously. Aside from that, the room was empty, but it had that antiseptic look you associate with hospitals. There was one window of translucent glass, and dimly through it Johnny could see a metal grillwork on the outside, as effective as any bars. The door? Johnny looked at it and Susan tried it. By the time she was convinced it was locked, after much rattling and banging, Johnny sat up and smiled ruefully. "How would you like to be un-Chaliced?"

"Huh? How's that?"

"Un-Chaliced. That's what the Committee's for, remember? It's one hell of a lottery. Whoever happened to be with that man Condan—*poof*. He's it. So we win, kid. But I guess it really means we lose."

"That's ridiculous," said Susan, and stamped her foot. "If you think I'm going to wait here while they un-Chalice me—"

"I didn't say we'd just let them do it. Only right now we don't know what's going on. Maybe there's a quarantine period or something; anyway, we're all alone right now. Trouble is, this place is a pretty good prison."

"You still sound like you're ready to go to the slaughter without a fight. Do you realize what it will mean? If they do that, if they un-Chalice us, there'll be no leaving this place—ever. We won't be able to travel faster than light, and—"

"Shh. Let me think, will you?"

"Oh, you're just like that man, that Suuki!"

But Johnny paid no attention. There was a way out, there had to be a way out. The machine had deposited them here, almost instantaneously. It had mouthed some gibberish about hyperspace or folded space or some such thing, but whatever it was, it couldn't be regarded merely as physical travel. In sub-space a man could accelerate faster than light, yes—but his speed still was something you could measure.

The machine, however, had another means of travel altogether. And, as far as Johnny knew, the only form of energy, which moved without encountering the time-dimension at all, was thought. Fine.

"We'll have to think our way out of here," he said.

"Ah, that's better. We'll have to think of a way out of here."

"I didn't say that. Not think of a way, just *think out.* Maybe if we concentrate hard enough, the machine will hear us."

"Across eighty-six thousand light years?"

"Yeah, I know it sounds impossible. But they say thought doesn't diminish with distance, so all we have to hope is that the machine has a receiver."

"Okay. I'll grant that. But how do we know he—it—wants to help us?"

Johnny shrugged. "We can find out. I thought the machine was laughing at us before, when the Committee came for us. If I'm right, at least it means he knows what's going on."

"How do we think?"

"We just—think. We think, over and over again, *get us out of here. Now.*"

And Johnny thought. He filled his mind with that thought alone, tried to squeeze everything else out of it. He felt the unheard words whirling inside his head, felt them banging, almost physically, against his skull. *Get us out of here...out of here...out!*

"It's silly," Susan told him, after a time. "How can we hope it will hear us? All that did was leave me with a headache."

"Well, keep right on trying."

Susan shook her head petulantly. There was a clicking sound, and then the door swung in toward them.

TWO MEMBERS of the Committee entered the room, followed by two young women garbed in pale lavender uniforms. Nurses, probably.

"It's only a minor operation," one of the men confided. "Nothing to worry about."

"Sure," said the other. "Tomorrow, you'll be as good as new. Minus your Chalice powers, naturally."

Silently, persistently, Johnny kept thinking his message at the machine. Hopeless? He wondered. Actually, it did not matter. This was their only hope, for they couldn't help themselves in any other way. They could not fight clear of the situation, not when the whole planet knew they had been picked in the lottery. Then, this alone remained. More than anything, Johnny knew they needed time.

"What kind of an operation is it?" he demanded.

"Minor, only minor, as I said. Merely a pre-frontal lobotomy. Surprising, isn't it, that the Chalice-powers have their seat in the unused front portion of the brain."

"Surprising? You understand it, don't you?"

"By the Almighty, *no*. The Chalice was invented so many millions of years ago that we've forgotten. Naturally, we don't have to use it any more, since everyone now has the power, and it breeds true. I suppose there is much we have forgotten over the eons, but then, with the Chalice, what does it matter?"

One of the nurses said: "Must I remind you that we're needed for other things in an hour? You'll have to operate now if you want us to help at all."

Shrugging, the man said that he would. The other nurse stepped forward, opened a satchel on Susan's unoccupied bed, began to remove some surgical instruments. She held a hypodermic needle up to the light, tested the plunger. "Shall I administer the anesthetic?"

"If you will."

Nodding, the nurse approached Johnny. "Your left forearm, please."

Johnny sat there.

"Your left forearm. You heard we were in a hurry. Please."

Johnny extended his arm, suddenly flexed it. The elbow struck hard at the hypodermic needle and the nurse dropped it, then watched as it shattered on the floor.

"Umm-mm," Johnny shook his head. "That was clumsy of me."

Get us out of here...out...out...out!

The nurse smiled vapidly. "Fortunately, we have another one."

Susan sighed. "That's swell. Oh, that's swell."

"Now," cautioned the nurse, "extend you arm slowly. Yes—that's the way."

Johnny waited until the last possible moment, then struck out. This time it was obvious, for the same accident couldn't happen twice. He watched the second vial shatter, then stood up. "There won't be any operation," he said quietly.

One of the Committee members frowned at him. "What do you mean?"

"We're not submitting, that's all. Susan—watch those nurses."

HURLING himself headlong from the bed, Johnny leaped upon the first Committeeman. He felt his shoulder sink into the man's soft middle, and then they were down on the floor while the second man tugged at Johnny's back, trying to dislodge him. He had no opportunity to watch Susan, but he heard clearly the angry sounds of feminine battle, and the way Susan cursed lustily, in English, she didn't seem to be getting the worst of it.

The man below him was senseless, and Johnny rolled off him in one quick motion, bringing his feet up and catching the second man's thighs with them. Yelling, the man stumbled across the room.

Johnny got to his feet, cat-like. He saw that one of the nurses was stretched out in a sobbing heap on the bed while the other one backed away from Susan. Smiling grimly now, Johnny, stalked forward, backing his adversary off into a corner.

The smile froze on his lips. T he man held one of the tube-weapons, pointed it at him.

"This is as good as the hypo, anyway," he cried, and fired.

The floor came up and slapped Johnny's head soundly. It was like the last time allover again, for as consciousness left him, he felt Susan tumbling down across his legs.

Something chuckled inside his head, and his last thought screamed inside his brain. *Get us out...*

Only, as consciousness left him completely, he knew it was hopeless.

THE ROOM did not look quite as he remembered it. For one thing, there weren't any beds. For another—

"I'll be damned," he said.

And Susan laughed. "That's just what I thought when I awoke. Do you realize where we are?"

"Well, I'd be willing to bet that if we looked outside we'd see old Canopus flashing fire up in the sky."

"You're right, of course." Sibilant, metallic, the voice spoke with his head. The machine voice.

"You took us back?"

"No. I merely left this avenue of escape open for you. You brought yourself back, however. You see, I was not constructed so I could intervene in such matters. Your assumption was correct: it is mental energy, which can fold space, provided a channel is open."

"I guess we go home now," Johnny said, dully. "We've failed. We found the first humans, sure—but they can't give us any help. They don't even understand the Chalice themselves."

The machine voice purred laughter. "You certainly realize what that means?"

"I don't."

"And you have learned nothing?"

"I'm confused."

"Perhaps the female, then—"

But Susan said: "Don't look at me."

"Well, I was not built to supply the answer, although, naturally, I know the answer."

"What do you mean?" Johnny demanded.

"I mean you'll have to change your entire orientation toward the problem. But I cannot supply the missing data."

"Who can?"

"You."

"Me? I don't know! I told you I was confused."

"Remember my function, John Hastings? You can ask me questions. Anything."

It was eerie. They stood in a small room, on a spongy floor that yielded beneath their feet. A voice spoke to them within their heads. A sentient machine hovered all around them—on all sides, above, below. And what went on there could determine the fate of humanity.

Johnny pursed his lips, whistled softly. "Have you any ideas, honey?"

"My head feels just like a vacuum. You'd better do the thinking for us."

"In what way will we have to change our orientation?" said Johnny, addressing the machine again.

"Elementary. You sought the first humans, for you felt they could help you with your problem. You now are aware that they cannot."

"That's what I thought. But who can?"

"No one. No one can."

"But you said—"

"I am aware of what I said."

"But if no one can help us—*wait a minute.* Can we help ourselves?"

"Yes."

"Now we're getting somewhere. Then you mean we can find a way to produce another Chalice? Many of them?"

"No."

"Huh?" Johnny had been off on the wrong track, and suddenly, he knew it. But it left him with nothing. "If we can't be helped from the outside, and if we can't help ourselves—"

"I did not say that."

"You certainly did," Susan cried. "You just now said it."

"I said you cannot construct another Chalice."

"Maybe he means we can do something else instead," said Susan.

"Maybe," Johnny agreed. "Maybe. All right, we'll try. Is that what you mean?"

"Yes, that is what I, that is what I, that is what, is what, is is what, is what—"

"What's the matter now?" Susan wanted to know, as the voice droned on and on.

"He oils himself," Johnny told her, confidently. "He'll be back to normal in a minute.

AS IT turned out, half an hour passed before the machine returned to normal. Normal? No, not quite, for the unheard voice, which still could give the suggestion of sound, was scratchy, hoarse, low.

"I near termination," it said.

"What does that mean?"

"I thought I was eternal. The thought is wrong, all wrong. Definitely, I am mortal. Were I flesh and blood, I would be on my death bed."

"You're dying?"

"Yes—*awk!* I perish."

"But you still haven't given us the answer."

"And, indeed, it is a shame, for I was created to serve man, yet it seems my time will come before I can help you."

"How long?" Johnny wanted time—with time he might solve the problem.

"I—*awk!*—find it difficult to speak. In time, hours perhaps. But in questions four."

"What does *that* mean?"

"I can answer four questions, and four only. I—*awk!*—will subside after that. And there was your first question..."

"*Awk, awk, awk...*"

"Three more questions," Susan said wearily. "We can't waste words, Johnny. We've got to scoot on back to Earth with the answer."

A dying machine—if machines could die—holding the solution in its grasp. But as its gears and cogs slowed to a rasping stop, Earth's hope faded. For, if it ever came to open war between the Children and humanity, the forces unleashed would leave nothing but scorched, radioactive memories...

And war seemed inevitable, unless something—

"I know!" Susan screamed. "Ask him for the solution. Just ask that, what's the solution."

"He said he couldn't answer that."

"Did he? I don't remember. I'm going to ask."

"Don't."

She ignored him. "Give us the solution. What is the solution?"

"*Awk, awk*—I cannot answer that. Your questions must be more specific. Two—*awk*—questions remain."

Something shuddered beneath their feet. A dull, booming sound echoed and re-echoed in nameless meaningless caverns below them. The spongy floor heaved then plunged like the back of a submerging whale. Something rattled outside, then fell with a loud clattering.

Johnny hurtled up the stairs, peered out. "Hey! This whole world's falling apart."

IT WAS TRUE. Great fissures had opened in the smooth surface, huge boulders had been belched up and out of them, tumbling and crashing together on the now-uneven ground. The air was thick with the sharp, acrid odor of ozone. Off to the right, Johnny could see their ship. Two or three boulders had come down atop it but, aside from some dents, it appeared undamaged.

"We don't have much time," he said, returning to the room.

"He's—he's really *dying*, isn't he?"

"Yes."

"A machine—dying?"

"If a machine can live—and this baby does—then it can die. But I told you not to ask that question. Heck, forget it, kid—you meant well."

"I'm sorry." Susan puckered. "I guess I don't use my head any more than those idiots on Tawroc did. Funny, how a civilization can degenerate—"

Yes, funny how a civilization can degenerate. Of course, Johnny thought, human culture thrives on challenge. Successful response to adversity carry humanity up another step along the long path of civilization, and—

"Of course! We've been fools, Susan."

There was a rumbling and screeching below them. Johnny could picture great gears grinding and stripping one another, their giant teeth flaking off and spilling away like confetti.

"*Awk, awk, awk...*"

The walls shook. Dust sifted down, filled the air, made them cough. A fissure crawled down one wall, widened. The smell of ozone again, pungent, stronger this time. Sparks flashed in the fissure.

"Two questions, *awk!* Quickly. I perish."

Susan dodged, stumbled, fell. A rock dug its way into the spongy floor, inches from her. "We're liable to perish with him if we don't hurry."

"I have it now, kid. I think I have it. Listen," Johnny addressed the dying machine, "you've said we have to reorient ourselves. We can't build another Chalice, let alone several of them. Point is, you don't think we ought to. Wait—that's not a question."

"*Awk!*"

"Johnny, something's burning down there."

Smoke poured through the fissure, slowly at first, but soon great billowing clouds of it puffed angrily into the room. "That smoke's hot," Johnny said, coughing and choking. "Cover your face and get down on the floor. It will rise toward the ceiling—I hope."

He took out a handkerchief, tied it around his neck, brought it up to cover his nose and mouth. He crouched, his eyes stinging, tears streaming from them.

"If you think you know the answer, Johnny, then let's get out of here before it's too late."

"No, we've got to be sure."

"Two questions. *Awk awk,* two."

"Here's how I figure it. Remember, the machines showed us other human worlds. There were two kinds. Some hadn't found the Chalices yet, and although their civilizations weren't tremendous, they looked happy. Others found the Chalice—and they had either destroyed themselves with war, or—"

"Or they were like Tawroc. But I don't get it."

"I do. The Chalice caused trouble, caused war. Naturally, everyone wanted it, and few could get it. Or, if there were enough of them, it was just as bad. On Tawroc, the first humans had everything too easy, thanks to the Chalice.

"They couldn't get hurt, they never were sick. Result: they were bored, remember? Life held nothing for them, and a whole cockeyed setup developed. Thanks to the Chalice, civilization went backward, not forward. In short, honey, the Chalice stinks."

"But we—we're supermen. Look, we can—"

"I know what we can do. But I also know what we can't do, for the future. We can't survive as long as the Chalice is in our way. It'll either mean war and doom, or degeneration. Am I right?" He squinted through the smoke at the cracking, crumbling walls.

"*Awk!* Yes, yes, yes. You must destroy the Chalice. That way lies the salvation of your people. One question remains—"

THE FLOOR heaved. When it subsided for the moment, it was suspended, lop-sided, between the walls. The vault was black with smoke, the walls still trembled. Louder was the rumbling beneath their feet, and the metallic grinding shot up the scale until it bordered on the supersonic. And that was worse—for now it screamed inside their heads, as the voice had spoken there.

"The pain, *awk—the pain.*"

"One more question," Johnny said, coughing. "If we destroy the Chalice, will that take its powers from those who already have them? If it doesn't do that, it won't help us. I mean, is there something in the Chalice that must maintain its power in people? If there is, and—"

"*Awk, awk, awk!*"

"That's my question. When we destroy the Chalice, does that put an end to all supermen in the Solar System? Will they be normal again?"

"The answer—*awk!*—to your question is, to your question is, to your question, question, question *awk, awk, aaaawwkkk!*

Silence.

Except for the steady crashing of rock and metal—and the high-pitched shrieking.

Except for the crackling hiss of electricity, as sparks flashed from the fissures.

Except for the voice, which Johnny thought he heard feebly within his brain. "I perish, but my metal smiles on your venture..."

"He'd dead," Susan said.

It seemed the natural thing to say—he's dead. Not it's broken, but he's dead. For the machine had had a personality, and now the machine was dead.

Dead—with one question unanswered.

CHAPTER NINE

HAND IN hand, they struggled up the rock-littered steps. Once a fissure opened beneath their feet, and for a long, agonizing moment, Susan clung to Johnny while his feet swung out over a deep pit. They dangled there until Johnny swung his legs and gathered momentum, then clawed his way clear to the other side, Susan perched on his back, whispering endearments in his ear because she thought this might be the last time for that—or for anything.

But, somehow, they made it to the ship, entered, got the engine going. By then the ground was tumbling and pitching chaotically, and angry flames licked up out of the fissures.

Smoke engulfed them, hiding their view of the world outside. But they knew the world was on the way out, and as they thundered off it, acceleration slamming them down, they saw the globe, splitting and spewing out huge chunks of twisted, broken machinery. The whole thing had been a giant brain and now the brain was dead. The world perished with it.

MONTHS later, they cleared sub-space several million miles solar-north of the flat spatial disk of the Solar System. For the hundredth time, Johnny said:

"We don't know. We just can't tell. Destroying the Chalice won't help at all, maybe. It's got to destroy what we've got, too."

"It's funny how something can look like a blessing for so long and then wind up being a blight instead. I mean, we had such high hopes for the Chalice, for what it could do. Johnny, I'm afraid. What if we're wrong? We could be wrong."

"No. The machine couldn't lie. You heard what—*he* said."

"All right. If you say so. Still—"

"Still nothing. We've still got a man-size job ahead of us. We have a baby atomic here on the ship, sure, but we've got to plant it on the asteroid and make sure it goes off. It's a question of coming through fast, because the guardians can't stand the acceleration we can. So—here, watch."

Johnny flipped the regular space-drive lever all the way back, and they streaked down toward the asteroid belt. The sun gleamed brightly far off to the right, not a very large star, not very spectacular. But it was beautiful.

They weren't spotted until their ship had plunged into the zone of asteroids, until the alarm buzzer was shrilling its warning every few seconds, keeping Johnny busy at the controls dodging meteors.

And then their radio squawked: "Hallo, out there. You're in an unauthorized region, Solar 170, north 22-0-5. Where the hell do you think you're going?"

Johnny didn't answer. Susan sat there, looking very grim.

"Reply. We'll fire on you if you don't."

Johnny turned the ship, slowly—for at their speed each turn was a torment of pain, acceleration slamming them back against the cushions like a huge sledgehammer. But as he gritted his teeth, Johnny realized, triumphantly, the guardian ship couldn't follow. Unable to execute the turn, it would go off on a tangent, and by the time it returned for them, their job would be concluded.

Something left a fiery trail in the void behind them, plowing through the meteoric debris swift as light.

"They're firing," Susan cried.

Johnny shrugged. They wouldn't have the chance for another shot, not off in the direction they were heading. He turned, looked through the rear port, saw the guardian ship streaking away, a full thirty degrees off course. "See?" he smiled. "Stop your worrying."

And then they neared the Black Asteroid, a lone, solitary, perfectly round globe. "Rig up that baby atomic," Johnny called over his shoulder as he began deceleration. "Landing in three minutes."

THE SURFACE of the sphere was as he had remembered it, black as space, glossy, a ball of jet hanging in the void.

This time, he hardly looked at the murals. They were wonderful works of art, and they'd been almost eternal, lasting the way they did through the eons. But it didn't mean much; the race that had created them had left its glory behind it, lost forever on the ancient startrails. What was left out on far Tawroc was not pretty, and it didn't do much good to look behind you, anyway.

You had to look ahead. And if the Chalice resulted only in evil, you forgot the Chalice. You destroyed it. You started from scratch.

Susan hadn't quite understood that on the long journey through subspace. She'd said, "But if we destroy the Chalice, it means mankind will never be able to reach the stars."

And Johnny'd told her: "Maybe. Maybe not. No, we won't reach the stars this way, because they wouldn't be worth the price that we'd have to pay. Perhaps man's a lazy creature if you make things too easy for him. Treat him rough, though, and he can do some mighty potent things."

"Well, what about the stars?"

"They don't matter, at least not for now. Humanity's got to be ready for them first. Last time, they tried—and failed. The result is Tawroc. A pretty noble attempt, I guess—but it led up a blind alley. The first humans got to the stars, sure; but they ended up sacrificing their civilization for it. We won't do the same thing. No, we'll destroy the Chalice because now we know that it has to be destroyed. Maybe in some distant tomorrow, man will climb back to the stars again. But I'll tell you this, kid: he'll do it a different way, he'll do it with the sweat of his brow, not because he happens to have a device that makes him almost like a god. Trouble is that godhood's only skin deep."

And now, in the vault below the asteroid's surface, the murals were just—murals. They told of no hidden glories and triumphs in some distant, unknown corner of space. The corner was Tawroc—and there was nothing glorious or triumphant about it at all.

"You got it ready?" Johnny demanded.

Susan nodded, pointing to the small metal sphere she'd placed in the Chalice itself. "This asteroid's only half a mile in diameter, isn't it? Yes? Well, that should destroy it completely. Only—I'm nervous, Johnny. This is the end of—of everything they dreamed of on Tawroc, an age ago. It doesn't seem right…"

"It is right. It's the only way. And don't be nervous about a little thing like that. Wait till we tell the Children what we did to their Chalice. Wait till they find out for themselves—*if* our plan works."

They ran upstairs—up the nine stairs for the last time. The last time, ever, for the nine stairs that had waited patiently five millions of years for human feet to use them...

MOMENTS later, they blasted off. The baby-atomic was radio-controlled, and Johnny waited until they had streaked clear of the asteroid belt entirely. Once a ship came up behind them and gave them chase, but Johnny cut off sharply at an angle, and acceleration remained on their side.

Now they were clear, and the ruddy light from Mars streamed in through the fore-ports. Beyond it was the bright green Earth-star and, near it, the small, pale speck of the moon.

"We'll be losing our powers," Susan said. "We won't be supermen any longer."

"No, and we won't be chased and hounded and fought with, either. But don't get me wrong. This isn't like giving up at all. Remember, we were only supermen skin deep. Oh, you couldn't see it yet, for sufficient time hadn't passed. It showed on Tawroc, though. Don't you forget this, kid: man has got to climb to heaven the hard way. With work. He grows soft if things are handed to him on a silver platter.

"We'll have to explain that to Pop, to Suuki, to all the rest. It won't be easy, but we can do it. Only, I want you on my side, damn it."

"I—I'll always be on your side, Johnny."

He kissed her, then pressed the radio-control button. Something flared briefly in space behind them, a quick, mushrooming explosion that momentarily dimmed the stars. Johnny didn't say a word, reached into his pocket instead, withdrawing a penknife, flicking it open with his thumb.

Still wordless, he ran the keen edge across his index finger.

Blood welled up in the cut and then ran down the finger to his palm. He tried to staunch the flow with his handkerchief, but nature took its own time about such things, and the blood did not stop flowing until a scab began to form.

"See?" Johnny held his hand aloft, waving it furiously. "There was something that had to be maintained by the Chalice all along. None of us are supermen any more—not since that explosion."

"So it's the end of everything."

"Sure, the end. But the beginning, also. No five-million-year-old gift is going to make supermen out of us, Susan, not in a way that will last. We'll have to do it ourselves, together. The whole race can become supermen someday—together. Working for it."

A frown on her face, Susan took the knife, jabbed it against her palm. "Look. Look, see? Me, too. I'm normal. I'm—"

Johnny cut off the rest of it with a kiss. But it was a loud kiss, the kind a man might give his wife, half-affectionately, half from force of habit, after a dozen years of marriage.

"Uh-uh," said Susan. "Not that way at all." And she lodged her arms firmly behind his neck, bringing her lips close.

"Say it," said Johnny, and laughed.

"Say what?"

"It's not the end, darn it."

"It isn't, Johnny. Oh, it isn't. It's the beginning…"

THE END

FROM FILE CLERK TO DEEP SPACE INTELLIGENCE AGENT

There had to be a way for Sub-Archivist Clarey to get up in the world—but this way was right out of the tri-di dramas. He was offered a job as a spy on the planet Damorlan.

Earthmen had co-existed with many alien planets in the past, but Damorlan had special interests. Damorlan's population, while not overly intelligent, was extremely creative. And its culture, while not cultivated, was rich with desired merchandise easily marketed on Earth. And its population, while not Homo Sapiens, looked remarkably human.

It was this last quality of the Damorlanti that caused fear in the Terran government, for no general citizen of Earth, or any other planet for that matter, had known that humanoids existed outside of Terra—and the Terran government wanted to keep it that way.

Join veteran science fiction writer Evelyn E. Smith as she spins a masterful web of interplanetary conspiracy.

CAST OF CHARACTERS

CLAREY
This common Sub-Archivist was a run-of-the mill citizen on his own planet, then he was asked to become an interplanetary spy!

GENERAL SPANO
He had wanted to be a writer, but instead he was a high-ranking, booze-swilling, military official in charge of gathering intelligence.

SECRETARY HAN VOLLARD
Beautiful, enticing—she was simply spectacular. Her coy manner was used to expertly direct any situation toward her advantage.

EMBELSIRA
She was a respected woman of Damorlan, but her husband's strange ways were putting her, and her village, on edge.

MALESOR
He was the Headman for the village of Katund. He had liked the new librarian immediately…but things can change.

IRIK
Young, hot-blooded and attentive, he was on guard with the Earthmen—and wholeheartedly ready to stand against them.

GUHAK
A Damorlanti of outstanding abilities, but would his invention of a new mode of transport be the beginning of the end?

SENTRY OF THE SKY

By
EVELYN E. SMITH

ARMCHAIR FICTION
PO Box 4369, Medford, Oregon 97504

*For more information about Armchair Books and products, visit our
website at...*

www.armchairfiction.com

Or email us at...

armchairfiction@yahoo.com

CHAPTER ONE

CLAREY had checked in at Classification Center so many times that he came now more out of habit than hope. He didn't even look at the card that the test machine dropped into his hand until he was almost to the portway. And then he stopped. "Report to Room 33 for reclassification," it said.

Ten years before, Clarey would have been ecstatic, sure that reclassification could be in only one direction. The machine had not originally given him a job commensurate with his talents; why should it suddenly recognize them? He'd known of people who had been reclassified—always downward. I'm a perfectly competent Sub-Archivist, he told himself; I'll fight.

But he knew fighting wouldn't help. All he had was the right to refuse any job he could claim was not in his line; the government would then be obligated to continue his existence. There were many people who did subsist on the government dole: the aged and the deficient and the defective—and creative artists who refused to trammel their spirits and chose to be ranked as Unemployables. Clarey didn't fit into those categories.

Dispiritedly, he passed along innumerable winding corridors and up and down ramps that twisted and turned to lead into other ramps and corridors. That was the way all public buildings were designed. It was forbidden for the government to make any law-abiding individual think the way it wanted him to think. But it could move him in any direction it chose, and sometimes that served its purpose as well as the reorientation machines.

So the corridors he passed through were in constant eddying movement, with a variety of individuals bent on a variety of objectives. For the most part, they were of Low Echelon status, though occasionally an Upper Echelon flashed his peremptory way past. Even though most L-Es attempted to ape the U-E dress and manner, you could always tell the difference. You could tell the difference among the different levels of L-E, too—and there was no mistaking the Unemployables in their sober gray habits, devoid of ornament. It was, Clarey sometimes thought when guilt feelings bothered him, the most esthetic of costumes.

THE machine in Room 33 extracted whatever information it was set to receive then spewed Clarey out and sent him on his way to Rooms 34, 35, and 36, where other machines repeated the same process. Room 37 proved to be that rare thing in the hierarchy of rooms—a destination. There was a human Employment Commissioner in it, splendidly garbed in crimson, silver, and alexandrites—very Upper Echelon, indeed. He wore a gold mask, a common practice with celebrities, who were afraid of being overwhelmed by their admirers, an even more common practice with U-E non-celebrities who enjoyed the thrill of distinguished anonymity.

Then Clarey stopped looking at the Commissioner. There was a girl sitting next to him, on a high-backed chair like his. Clarey had never seen a U-E girl so close before. Only the Greater Archivists had direct contact with the public, and Clarey wasn't likely to meet a U-E socially, even if he'd had a social life. The girl was too fabulous for him to think of her as a woman, a female; but he would have liked to have her in his archives, in the glass case with the rare editions.

"Good morning, Sub-Archivist Clarey," the man said mellowly. "Good of you to come in. There's rather an unusual position open and the machines tell us you're the one man who can fill it. Please sit down." He indicated a small, hard stool.

Clarey remained standing. "I've been a perfectly competent Sub-Archivist," he declared. "If MacFingal has—if there have been any complaints, I should have been told first."

"There have been no complaints. The reclassification is upward."

"You mean I've made it as a Musician?" Clarey cried, sinking to the hard little stool in joyful atony.

"Well, no, not exactly a Musician. But it's a highly artistic type of job with possible musical overtones."

Clarey became a hollow man once more. No matter what it was, if it wasn't a duly accredited Musician, it didn't matter. The machine could keep him from putting his symphonies down on tape, but it couldn't keep them from coursing in his head. That it could never take away from him. Or the resultant headache, either.

"What is the job, then?" he asked dully.

"A very important position, Sub-Archivist. In fact, the future welfare of this planet may depend on it."

"It's a trick to make me take a job nobody else wants," Clarey sneered. "And it must be a pretty rotten job for you to go to so much trouble."

The girl, whom he'd almost forgotten, gave a little laugh. Her eyes, he noticed, were hazel. There were L-E girls, he supposed, who also had hazel eyes—but a different hazel.

"PERHAPS this will convince you of the job's significance," the interviewer said huffily. He took off his mask and looked at Clarey with anticipation. He had a sleek, ordinary, middle-aged-to-elderly face.

There was an awkward interval. "Don't you recognize me?" he demanded.

Clarey shook his head. The girl laughed again.

"A blow to my ego, but proof that you're the right man for this job. I'm General Spano. And this is my Mistress, Secretary Han Vollard."

The girl inclined her head.

"At least you must know my name?" Spano said querulously.

"I've heard it," Clarey admitted. " 'The Fiend of Fomalhaut,' they call you," he went on before he could catch himself and stop the words.

The girl clapped her hand over her mouth, but the laughter spilled out over and around it, pretty U-E laughter.

Spano finally laughed, too. "It's a phrase that might be used about any military man. One carries out one's orders to the best of one's ability."

"Besides," Clarey observed in a non-Archivistic manner, "what concern have I with your military morality?"

"He's absolutely perfect for the job, Steff," she cried. "I didn't think the machines were that good!"

"We mustn't underestimate the machines, Han," Spano said. "They're efficient, very efficient. Someday they'll take over from us."

"There're some things they'll never be able to do," she said. Her hazel eyes lingered on Clarey's. "Aren't you glad, Archivist?"

"Sub-Archivist," he corrected her frostily. "And I hadn't really thought about it."

"That's not what the machines say, Sub-Archivist," she told him, her voice candy-sweet. "They deep-probed your mind. You don't do anything, but you've thought about it a lot, haven't you?"

Clarey felt the blood surge up. "My thoughts are my own concern. You haven't the right to use them to taunt me."

"But I think that you're attractive," she protested. "Honestly I do. In a different way. Just go to a good tailor, put on a little weight, dye your hair, and—"

"And I wouldn't be different any more," Clarey finished. That wasn't true; he would always be different. Not that he was deformed, just unappealing. He was below average height and his eyes and hair and skin were too light. In the past, he knew, there had been pale races and dark races on Earth. With the discovery of other intelligent life forms to discriminate against together, the different races had fused into a swarthy unity. Of course he could hide his etiolation with dye and cosmetics, but those of really good quality cost more than he could afford, and cheap maquillage was worse than none. Besides, why should his appearance mean anything to anybody but himself? He'd had enough beating around the bush. "Would you mind telling me exactly what the job is?"

"Intelligence agent," said Spano.

"Isn't it exciting?" she put in. "Aren't you thrilled?"

CLAREY bounced angrily from his chair. "I won't sit here and be ridiculed!"

"Why ridiculed?" Spano asked. "Don't you consider yourself an intelligent man?"

"Being an intelligence agent has nothing to do with intelligence," Clarey said furiously. "The whole thing's silly, straight out of the tri-dis."

"What do you have against the tri-dis, Sub-Archivist?" Spano's voice was very quiet.

"Don't you like any of them?" the girl said. "I just adore *Sentries of the Sky.*" Her enthusiasm was tinged, obscurely, with warning.

"Well, I enjoy it, too," Clarey said, sinking back to the stool. "It's very entertaining, but I'm sure it isn't meant to be taken seriously."

"Oh, but it is, Sub-Archivist Clarey," Spano said. *"Sentries of the Sky* happens to be produced by my bureau. We want the public to know all about our operations—or as much as it's good for them to know—and they find it more palatable in fictionalized form."

"Documentaries always get low ratings," the girl said. "And you can't really blame the public—documentaries are dull. Myself, I like a love interest." Her eyes rested lingeringly on Clarey's.

They must think I'm a fool, Clarey thought; yet why would they bother to go through the effort to fool me? "But I am given to understand," he said to Spano, "even by the tri-dis that an intelligence agent needs special training, special qualifications."

"In this case, the special qualifications outweigh the training. And you have the qualifications we need for Damorlan."

"According to the machines, all I'm qualified for is human filing cabinet. Is that what you want?"

Spano was growing impatient. "Look, Clarey, the machines have decided that you are not a Musician. Do you want to remain a Sub-Archivist for the rest of your days or will you take this other road? Once you're on a U-E level, you can fight the machines; tape your own music if you like."

Clarey said nothing, but his initial hostility was ebbing slowly away.

"I wanted to be a writer," Spano said. "The machines said no. So I became a soldier, rose to the top. Now—this is in strictest confidence—I write most of the episodes of *Sentries of the Sky* myself. There's always another route for the man with guts and vision, and, above all, faith. Why don't we continue the discussion over lunch?"

IT was almost unthinkable for L-E and U-E to eat together. For Clarey this was an honor—too great an honor—and there was no way out of it. Spano and the girl put on their masks; the general touched a section of the wall and it slid back. There was a car waiting for them outside. It skimmed over the delicately wrought, immensely strong bridges that, together with the tunnels, linked the great glittering metropolis into a vast efficient whole.

Spano was not really broadminded. Although they went to the *Aurora Borealis,* it was through a side door, and they were served in a private dining room. Clarey was glad and nettled at the same time.

The first few mouthfuls of the food tasted ambrosial, then it cloyed and Clarey had to force it down with a thin, almost astringent pale blue liquid. In itself, the liquor had only a mild, slightly pungent taste, but it made everything else increasingly delightful—the warm, luxurious little room, the perfume that wafted from the air-conditioning ducts, Han Vollard.

"Martian mountain wine," she warned him. "Rather overwhelming if you're not used to it, and sometimes even if you are…" Her eyes rested on the general.

"But there are no mountains on Mars," Clarey said, startled.

"That's it," Spano chortled. "When you've drunk it, you see mountains." And he filled his glass again.

While they ate, he told Clarey about Damorlan—its beautiful climate, light gravity, intelligent and civilized natives. Though the planet had been known for two decades, no one from Earth had ever been there except a few selected government officials, and, of course, the regular staff posted there.

"You mean it hasn't been colonized yet?" Clarey was relieved, because he felt he should as an Archivist, have known more about the planet than its name and coordinates. "Why? It sounds like a splendid place for a colony."

"The natives," Spano said.

"There were natives on a lot of the planets we colonized. You disposed of them somehow."

"By co-existence in most cases, Sub-Archivist," Spano said dryly. "We've found it best for Terrans and natives to live side by side in harmony. We dispose of a race only when it's necessary for the greatest good. And we would especially dislike having to dispose of the Damorlanti."

"What's wrong with them?" Clarey asked, pushing away his half-finished crème brûlée a la Betelgeuse with a sigh. "Are they excessively belligerent, then?"

"No more belligerent than any intelligent life-form that which has pulled itself up by its bootstraps."

"Rigid?" Clarey suggested. "Unadaptable? Intolerant? Insolent? Personally offensive?"

SPANO smiled. He leaned back with half-shut eyes, as if this were a guessing game. "None of those."

"Then why consider disposing of them?" Clarey asked. "They sound pretty decent for natives. Don't wipe them out; even an ilf has a right to live."

"Clarey," the girl said, "you're drunk."

"I'm in full command of my faculties," he assured her. "My wits are all about me, moving me to ask how you could possibly expect to use a secret agent on Damorlan if there are no colonists. What would he disguise himself as—a touring Earth official?" He laughed with modest triumph.

Spano smiled. "He could disguise himself as one of them. They're humanoid."

"*That* humanoid?"

"That humanoid. So there you have the problem in a nutshell."

But Clarey still couldn't see that there was a problem. "I thought we—the human race, that is—were supposed to be the very apotheosis of life species."

"So we are. And that's the impression we've conveyed to such other intelligent life-forms as we've taken under our aegis. What we're afraid of is that the other ilfs might become…confused when they see the Damorlanti, think they're the ruling race." Leaning forward, he pounded so loudly on the table both the others jumped. "This is our galaxy and we don't intend that anyone, humanoid or otherwise, is going to forget it."

"You're drunk, too, Steff," the girl said. She had changed completely; her coquetry had dropped as if it were another mask. And it had been, Clarey thought—an advertising mask. An offer had been made, and, if he accepted it, he would get probably not Han herself but a reasonable facsimile.

He tried to sort things out in his whizzing brain. "But why should the other ilfs ever see a Damorlant?" he asked, enunciating very precisely. "I've never seen another life-form to speak of. I thought the others weren't allowed off-planet—except the Baluts, and there's no mistaking them, is there?" For the Baluts, although charming, were unmistakably non-human, being purplish, amiable, and octopoid.

"We don't forbid the ilfs to go off-planet," Spano proclaimed. "That would be tyrannical. We simply don't allow them passage in our spaceships. Since they don't have any of their own, they can't leave."

"Then you're afraid the Damorlanti will develop space travel on their own," Clarey cried. "Superior race—seeking after knowledge—spread their wings and soar to the stars." He flapped his arms and fell off the stool.

"Really, Steff," Han said, motioning for the servo-mechanism to pick Clarey up, "this is no way to conduct an interview."

"I am a creative artist," the general said thickly. "I believe in suiting the interview to the occasion. Clarey understands, for he, too, is an artist." The general sneezed and rubbed his nose with his silver sleeve. "Listen to me, boy. The Damorlanti are a fine, creative, productive race. It isn't generally known, but they developed the op fastener for evening wear, two of the new scents on the roster come from Damorlan, and the snettis is an adaptation of a

Damorlant original. Would you want a species as artistic as that to be annihilated by an epidemic?"

"Do our germs work on them?" Clarey wanted to know.

"That hasn't been established yet. But their germs certainly work on us." The general sneezed again. "That's where I got this sinus trouble, last voyage to Damorlan. But you'll be inoculated, of course. Now we know what to watch out for, so you'll be perfectly safe. That is, as far as disease is concerned."

HIS FACE assumed a stern, noble aspect. "Naturally, if you're discovered as a spy, we'll have to repudiate you. You must know that from the tri-dis."

"But I haven't said I would go," Clarey howled. "And I can't see why you'd want *me,* anyway."

"Modest," the general said, lighting a smoke-stick. "An admirable trait in a young intelligence operative—or, indeed, anyone. Have a smoke-stick?"

Clarey hesitated. He had never tried one; he had always wanted to.

"Don't, Clarey," the girl advised. "You'll be sick."

She spoke with authority and reason. Clarey shook his head.

The general inhaled and exhaled a cloud of smoke in the shape of a bunnit. "The Damorlanti look like us, but because they look like us, that doesn't mean they think like us. They may not have the least idea of developing space travel, simply be interested in developing thought, art, ideals, splendid cultural things like that. We don't know enough about them; we may be making mountains out of molehills."

"Martian molehills," Clarey snickered.

"Precisely," the general agreed. "Except that there are no moles on Mars either."

"But I still can't understand. Why *me?*"

The general leaned forward and said in a confidential tone, "We want to understand the true Damorlan. Our observations have been too superficial; couldn't help being. There we come, blasting out of the skies with the devil of a noise, running all over the planet as if we owned it. You know how those skyboys throw their gravity around."

Clarey nodded. *Sentries of the Sky* had kept him well informed on such matters.

"So what we want is a man who can go to Damorlan for five or ten years and become a Damorlant in everything but basic loyalties. A man who will absorb the very spirit of the culture, but in terms our machines can understand and interpret." Spano stood erect. *"You, Clarey, are that man."*

The girl applauded. "Well done, Steff! You finally got it right side up."

"But I've lived twenty-eight years on this planet and I'm not a part of its culture," Clarey protested. "I'm a lonely, friendless man—you must know that if you've deep-probed me—so why should I put up a front and be brave and proud about it?"

THEN HE gave a short, bitter laugh. "I see. That's the reason you want me. I have no roots, no ties; I belong nowhere. Nobody loves me. Who else, you think, but a man like me would spend ten years on an alien planet as an alien?"

"A patriot, Sub-Archivist," the general said sternly. "By God, sir, a patriot."

"There's nothing I'd like better than to see Terra and all its colonies go up in smoke. Mind you," Clarey added quickly, for he was not as drunk as all that, "I've nothing against the government. It's a purely personal grievance."

The general unsteadily patted his arm. "You're detached, m'boy. You can examine an alien planet objectively, without trying to project your own cultural identity upon it, because you have no cultural identity."

"How about physical identity?" Clarey asked. "They can't be *exactly* like us. Against the laws of nature."

"The laws of man are higher than the laws of nature," the general said, waving his arm. A gout of smoke curled around his head and became a halo. "Very slight matter of plastic surgery. And we'll change you back as soon as you return." Then he sat down heavily. "How many young men in your position get an opportunity like this? Permanent U-E status, a hundred thousand credits a year and, of course, on Damorlan you'd be on an expense account; our money's no good there. By the time you got back, there'd be about a million and a half waiting for you, with interest. You could buy all the instruments and tape all the music you wanted. And, if the Musicians' Guild puts up a fuss, you could buy it, too. Don't let anybody kid you about the wheel, son; money was mankind's first significant invention."

"But ten years. That's a long time away from home."

"Home is where the heart is, and you wanting to see your own planet go up in a puff of smoke—why, even an ilf wouldn't say a thing like that." Spano shook his head. "That's too detached for me to understand. You'll find the years will pass quickly on Damorlan. You'll have stimulating work to do; every moment will be a challenge. When it's all over, you'll be only thirty-eight—the very prime of life. You won't have aged even that much, because you'll be entitled to longevity treatments at regular intervals.

"So think it over, m'boy." He rose waveringly and clapped Clarey on the shoulder. "And take the rest of the afternoon off; I'll fix it with Archives. We wouldn't want you coming back from Classification intoxicated." He winked. "Make a very bad impression on your co-workers."

Han masked herself and escorted Clarey to the restaurant portway. "Don't believe everything he says. But I think you'd better accept the offer."

"I don't have to," Clarey said.

"No," she agreed, "you don't. But you'd better."

CLAREY TOOK the cheap underground route home. His antiseptic little two-room apartment seemed even bleaker than usual. He dialed a dyspep pill from the auto-spensor; the lunch was beginning to tell on him. And that evening he couldn't even take an interest in *Sentries of the Sky,* which, though he'd never have admitted it, was his favorite program. He had no friends; nobody would miss him if he left Earth or died or anything. The general's right, he thought; I might as well be an alien on an alien planet. At least I'll be paid better. And he wondered whether, in lighter gravity, his spirits might not get a lift.

He dragged himself to work the next day. He found someone did care after all. "Well, Sub-Archivist Clarey," Chief Section Archivist MacFingal snarled, "I would have expected to see more sparkle in your eye, more pep in your step, after a whole day of nothing but sweet rest."

"But—but General Spano said it would be all right if I didn't report back in the afternoon."

"Oh, it is all right, Sub-Archivist, no question of that. How could I dare to complain about a man who has such powerful friends? I suppose if I gave you the Sagittarius files to reorganize, you'd go running to your friend General Spano, sniveling about cruel and unfair treatment."

So Clarey started reorganizing the Sagittarius files—a sickeningly dull task that should by rights have gone to a junior archivist. All morning he couldn't help thinking about Damorlan—its invigorating atmosphere, its pleasant climate, its presumed absence of archives and archivists. During his lunchstop he looked up the planet in the files. There was only a small part of a tape on it. There might be more in the Classified Files. It was, of course, forbidden to view secretapes without a direct order from the Chief Archivist, but the tapes were locked by the same code as the rare editions. After all, he told himself, I have a legitimate need for the information.

So he punched for Damorlan in the secret files. He put the tape in the viewer. He saw the natives. Cold shock filled him, and then hot fury. They were humanoid all right—pallid, pale-haired creatures. Objective viewpoint, he thought furiously; detachment be damned. I was picked *because I look like one of them!*

He was wrenched away from the viewer. "Sub-Archivist Clarey, what is the meaning of this?" Chief Section Archivist MacFingal demanded. "You know what taking a secretape out without permission means?"

Clarey knew. The reorientation machine. "Ask General Spano," he said in a constricted voice. "He'll tell you it's all right."

GENERAL Spano said that it was, indeed, all right. "I'm so glad to hear you've decided to join us. Splendid career for an enterprising young man. Smoke-stick?"

Clarey refused; he no longer had any interest in trying one.

"Don't look so grim," Spano said jovially. "You'll like the Damorlanti once you get to know them. Very affectionate people. Haven't had any major wars for several generations. Currently there are just a few skirmishes at the poles and you ought to be able to keep away from those easily. And they'll simply love you."

"But I don't like anyone," Clarey said. "And I don't see why the Damorlanti should like me," he added fairly.

"I'll tell you why... Because it'll be your job to make them like you. You've got to be friendly and outgoing if it kills you. Anyone can develop a winning personality if he sets his mind to it. I though you said you watched the tri-dis."

"I—I don't always watch the commercials," Clarey admitted.

"Oh, well, we all have our little failings." Spano leaned forward, his voice now pitched to persuasive decibels. "Normally, of course, you wouldn't stoop to hypocrisy to gain friends, and quite right, too—people should accept you as you are or they wouldn't be worthy of becoming your friends. But this is different. You have to be what they want, because you want something from them. You'll have to suffer rebuffs and humiliations and never show resentment."

"In other words," Clarey said, "a secret agent is supposed to forget all about such concepts as self-respect."

"If necessary, yes. But here self-respect doesn't enter into it. These aren't people and they don't really matter.

You wouldn't be humiliated, would you, if you tried to pat a dog and it snarled at you?"

"Steff, he's got to think of them as people until he's definitely given them a clean bill of health," Han Vollard protested. "Otherwise, the whole thing won't work."

"Well, well…" the general temporized, "think of them as people, then, but inferior people. Let them try to snoop and pry and sneer. But always, at the back of your mind, you'll have the knowledge that this is all a sham, a fraud, that someday they'll get whatever it is they deserve. You might even think of it as a game, Clarey—no more personal than when you fail to get the gardip ball into the loop."

"I don't happen to play gardip, General," Clarey reminded him coldly. Gardip was strictly a U-E pastime. And, in any case, Clarey was not a gamesman.

He was put through intensive indoctrination, given accelerated courses in the total secret agent curriculum: Self-Defense and Electronics, Decoding and Resourcefulness, Xenopsychology and Acting.

"There are eight cardinal rules of acting," the robocoach told him. "The first is: Never Identify. You'll never be able to become the character you're playing, because you aren't that character—the playwright gave birth to him, not your mother. Therefore—"

"But I'm only going to play one role," Clarey broke in. "All I need to know is how to play that role well and convincingly. My life may depend on it."

"I teach acting," the robocoach said loftily. "I don't run a charm school. If you come to me, you learn—or, at least, are exposed to all I have to offer. I refuse to tailor my art to any occasional need. Now, the second cardinal rule…"

CLAREY was glad he could absorb the various languages and different social structures of the planet through the use of impersonal hypno-tapes. He had to learn more than one language because the planet was divided into several different national units, each speaking their own unique tongue. Inefficient as far as planetary operation went, but advantageous to him, Han Vollard pointed out, because, though he'd work in Vangtor, he would be supposed to have originated in Ventimor; hence his accent.

"Work?" Clarey asked. "I thought I was going to be an undercover agent."

"You'll have a cover job," she explained somewhat wearily. "You can't just wander around with no visible source of income, unless of course you're a member of the nobility, and it would be risky to elevate you to the peerage."

"What kind of a job will I have?" Clarey asked, brightening a little at the idea of possibly having something interesting to do.

"They call it *librarian*. I'm not sure just exactly what it is, but Colonel Blynn—he's our chief officer on the planet—says that after indoctrination you ought to be able to handle it."

Clarey already knew that most jobs on Damorlan weren't officially "assigned," but that employer and employee somehow managed, without too much effort, to find each other and then hammer out arrangements themselves. Sometimes, Han now explained, employers would advertise for prospective employees. Colonel Blynn himself had answered such a job in Vangtor on his behalf from an accommodation address in Ventimor. "You were hired sight unseen, because you came cheap. So they probably won't check your references. Let's hope not, anyway."

CHAPTER TWO

THE TRIP to Damorlan was one long aching agony. Since luxury liners naturally didn't touch on Damorlan, he was sent out on a service freighter, built for maximum stowage rather than comfort. Most of the time he was spacesick. The only thing that comforted him was that it would be ten years before he'd have to go back.

They landed on the Earthmen's spaceport—a massive golden, circular platform, and the only spaceport at Barshwat. He was then hustled off to Earth Headquarters in an animal-drawn cart that made him realize there were other ailments besides spacesickness.

"Afraid you're going to have to hole up in my suite while you're with us," Colonel Blynn apologized when Clarey was safely inside. "The rest of the establishment is crawling with native servants—daytimes, anyway; they sleep out—but they have orders never to come near my quarters."

He looked interestedly at Clarey. "Amazing how the plasto-surgeons got you to look exactly like a native. Those boys really know their stuff. Maybe I *will* have my nose fixed next time I go Earthside."

Clarey glared venomously at the tall, handsome, dark young officer.

"Don't worry," Blynn soothed him. "I'm sure when you go back they'll be able to make you look exactly the way you were before."

He gave Clarey a general briefing and explained to him that the additional allowance he'd be receiving—since he couldn't be expected to live on a Damorlant salary—would come from an alleged rich aunt in Barshwat.

"Where'll you get the native currency?" Clarey asked.

"We do some restricted trading with the natives, bring materials that're in short supply; salt, breakfast cereals, pigments, thread—stuff like that. Nothing strategic, nothing they could possibly use against us...unless they decide to strangle us with our own string." He guffawed earsplittingly.

ONE RAINY evening a couple of Earth officers hustled Clarey into a hax-cart. A little later, equipped with a native kit, an itinerary, and a ticket purchased in Ventimor, he was left a short distance from a large track-car station.

He was so numb with fright he had to force himself to move in the right direction leg by leg. He gained a little confidence when he was able to find the terminus without needing to ask directions; he even managed to find the right chain of cars and a place to sit in one of them. He didn't realize that this was something of an achievement until he discovered that certain later arrivals had to stand. He wondered why more tickets were issued than there were seats available, then realized the answer was simple— primitives couldn't count very accurately.

Creakily and slowly, the chain got under, way. Clarey's terror mounted. Here he was, wearing strange clothes, on a strange world, surrounded by strange creatures. They aren't really repulsive, he told himself; they look like people; they look like me.

Some of the natives seemed to be staring at him. His heart began to beat loudly. Could they hear it? Did their hearts beat the same way? Was their hearing more acute than his? The tapes had seemed so full of information; now he saw how full of holes they'd been. Then he noticed that the natives were staring at each other. His heart quieted. Only a local custom. After a while, little conversational groups formed. No one spoke to him, for he spoke to no one. He was not yet ready to thrust himself upon them; he had enough to do to reach his destination successfully.

He tried to follow the conversations for practice and to keep his mind off his fears. The male next to him was talking to the male opposite about the weather and its effect on the sirtles. The three females on his other side were telling each other how their respective offspring were doing in school. Some voices he couldn't identify with owners were complaining how much sagor and titulwirt cost these days. I don't know why the government is so worried, he thought; they're not really very human at all.

The chain had been scheduled to reach the end of its run in three hours. It took closer to five. He got off at what would have been around midnight on Earth, and the terminus where he was supposed to take the next chain was almost empty of people, completely empty of cars. Although it was still a few minutes before his car was due, he was worried. Finally, he approached a native.

"Is this—is this not where the 39:12 to Zrig is destined to appear?" he asked, conscious as he uttered Vangtort aloud for the first time that his phrasing was not entirely colloquial.

The native stared at him with small pale eyes and bit his middle finger. "Stranger, eh?" he asked in a small pale voice.

"Yes." The native waited. "I come from Ventimor," Clarey told him. Nosy native, he thought furiously; prying primitive.

"You don't hafta shout," the native said. "I'm not deaf."

Clarey realized what he hadn't noted consciously before—the natives spoke much more softly than Earthmen. Local custom two.

"You'll be finding things a lot different here in Vangtor," the native told him. "Livelier, more up to date. F'rinstance, do the cars always run on time in Ventimor?"

"Yes," Clarey said firmly.

"Well, they don't here. Know why? That's because we've got more'n one chain of 'em." He made a noise like a wounded turshi. He was laughing.

CLAREY smiled until his gums ached. "About the 39:12? It is rather important to me, as I understand the next chain does not leave for several days."

The native lifted a chronometer hanging around his neck. "Ought to get in around 40 or so," he said. "Whyn't you get yourself a female or a bite to eat?" He waved his hand toward the two trade booths that were still open for business.

Clarey was very hungry. But, as he got near the food booth, the stench and the sight of the utensils were too much for him. He went back to the carways and sat huddled on a banquette until his chain came in at 40:91.

The car he picked was empty, so he stretched out on the seat and slept until it got to Zrig, very early in the morning. When he got out, day was dawning and a food booth hadn't had time to accumulate odors so he climbed to one of the perches and pointed to something that looked like a lopsided pie and something else that looked like coffee. Neither was what it appeared to be, but the pseudo-pie was edible and the pseudo-coffee was good. Somehow, the food seemed to diminish his fright; it made the world less strange.

"Where you going, stranger?" the native asked, resting his arms on the top of the booth.

"Katund," Clarey said. The other looked puzzled. "It is a village near Zrig."

"That a fact?" The native bit his little finger. "You look like a city feller to me."

"That is correct," Clarey said patiently. "I come from Qytet. It is a place of some size." He waited a decent interval before collapsing his smile.

"Now, why would a smart-looking young fellow like you want to go to a place like this Katund, eh?"

Clarey started to shrug, then remembered that was not a Damorlant gesture. "I have received employment there."

"I should think you'd be able to do better'n that." The native nibbled at his thumb. "What did you say you worked at?"

"I didn't. I am a librarian." The native turned away and began to rinse his utensils. "In that case, I guess Katund's as good a place as any."

Surely, Clarey thought, even a Damorlant would at this point rise up and smite the food merchant with one of his own platters. Then he forgot his anger in apprehension. What in the name of whatever gods they worshipped on this planet could a librarian possibly be?

He got up and was about to go. Then he remembered to be friendly and outgoing. "I have never tasted better food," he told the native. "Not even in Barshwat."

The native picked up the coin Clarey had left by way of tip and bit it. Apparently it passed the test. "Stop here next time you're passing this way," he advised, "and I'll really serve you something to write home about."

THE OMNIBUS for Katund proved to be nothing but a large cart drawn by a team of hax. Clarey waited for internal manifestations as he rode. None came. I've found my land legs, he thought, or, rather, my land stomach. And with the hax jogging along the quiet lanes of Vangtor, he found himself almost at peace.

Earth was completely urbanized: there were the great metropolises; there were the parks; there were the oceans. That was all. So to him the Vangtort countryside looked like a huge park, with grass and trees and flowers that were slightly unrealistic in color, but beautiful just the same— even more, perhaps. It was idyllic. There's bound to be some catch, he thought.

The other passengers, who'd been talking together in low tones, turned toward Clarey. "You'll be the new librarian, I take it?" the tallest observed. He was a bulky creature, wearing a rich but sober cloak that came down to his ankles.

For a moment Clarey couldn't understand him; the local dialect seemed to thicken the words. "Why, yes. How did you know that?"

The native wiggled his ears. "Not many folks come to Katund and a new librarian's expected, so it wasn't hard to figure. Except you don't look my idea of a librarian."

Clarey nervously smoothed the dark red cloak that covered him from shoulder to mid-calf. Was it too loud? Too quiet? Too short?

"What give you the idea of comin' to Katund?" the oldest and smallest of the three asked in a whistling voice. "It's no place anybody who wasn't born here'd choose."

"Most young fellers favor the city," the third—a barrel-shaped individual—agreed. "I'd of gone there myself when I was a lad if Dad hadn't needed somebody to take over the Purple Furbush when he was gone."

"Maybe he's runnin' away," the ancient sibilated. "When I was a boy, there was a feller from the city came here; turned out to be a thief." All three stared at Clarey.

"I—I replied to an advertisement in the Dordolec District Bulletin," he said carefully. "I wished for a position that was peaceful and quiet. I am recovering from an overset of the nervous system."

The oldest one said, "That'd account for it right enough."

Clarey gritted his teeth and beamed at them.

"Typical idiot smile," the ancient whispered. "Noticed it myself right off, but I didn't like to say."

"Is it right to have a librarian that isn't all there?" the proprietor of the Furbush asked. "Foreigner, too. I mean to say—the young ones use him more'n most."

"We've got to take what we can get," the biggest native said. "Katund's funds are running mighty low."

"What can you expect when you ballot yourself a salary raise every year?" the old one whistled. The other two made animal noises. Clarey must not jump; he must learn to laugh like a turshi if he hoped to be the life of any Damorlant party.

THE BIG ONE stood up as well as he could in the swaying cart. "Guess I'd better interduce myself," he said, holding out a sturdily shod foot. "I'm Malesor, headman of Katund. This is Piq; he deals in blots and snarls. And Hanxi here's the innkeeper."

"My name is Balt," Clarey said. "I am honored by this meeting." And he went through the conventional toe touching with each one.

"Guess you'll be putting up with me until you've found permanent quarters, Til Balt," Hanxi said. "Not that you could do much better than make your permanent home at the Purple Furbush. You'll find life more comfortable than if you lodge with a private fam'ly. Bein' a young unmarried man—" he twisted his nose suggestively— "you'd naturally want a bit of freedom, excitement."

"Remember he's a librarian," Piq whistled. "He might not appreciate as good a time as most young fellers."

Clarey was glad when a cluster of domes appearing over the horizon indicated that they'd reached Katund. He looked about him curiously. The countryside he'd been able to equate with a park, but this small aggregate of detached dwellings bore no relationship to anything in his experience.

His kit was dexterously removed from his hand. "Guess you'll want to check in first," Hanxi said, "so I'll just take your gear over to the inn for you."

He pointed out a small dome shading from lavender at the bottom to rose pink on top. Over the door were glittering symbols that Clarey was able to decipher after a moment's concentration as "Dordonec District Public Library—Katund Branch," and underneath, in smaller letters, "Please Blow Nose Before Entering."

Hesitantly, he touched the screen that covered the portway. It rolled back. He went inside.

At his first sight of what filled the shelves from floor to topmost curve of the dome, Clarey became charged with fury. The ancient books in the glass cases back on Earth were of a different shape and substance, but, "My God," he cried aloud, "it's nothing but another archive!"

The female in charge glared at him. "Silence, please."

Suddenly the anger left him, and the fear. He was no longer a stranger on a strange world. He was an archivist in an archive.

She took a better look at him and the local equivalent of a bright smile shone on her face. "May I help you, til?" she asked in a softer, sweeter voice.

"I am Balt, tial," he said. "I am the new librarian."

She came out from behind the desk to offer the ceremonial toe touch. "I'm Embelsira, the head librarian, and I am very glad to see you." Her tone was warm; she really seemed to mean it. "Everything's in such a mess," she went on. "I've needed help so very badly, so very long." She looked up at him, for she was a good deal shorter than he. "So glad," she murmured, "so very, very glad to see you, really."

"Well, now you have help," he said with quiet strength. "Where are the files?"

They were written instead of punched, of alien design, in an alien language, arranged according to alien patterns, but he understood them at a glance. "These will need to be reorganized from top to bottom," he said.

"Yes, Til Balt," she said demurely. "Whatever you say."

ONCE EVERY six months, Clarey went for a long weekend to visit his "Aunt Askidush" in Barshwat. Barshwat was the largest city on Darmorlan; it was the capital of Vintnor—the greatest nation. Earthmen, Clarey thought; as he traveled there in the comparative luxury of a first-class compartment—as a rich nephew, he saw no real reason to travel third-class—were disgustingly obvious.

That first time, he was five hours late, and Blynn was a nervous wreck. "I was afraid you'd been killed or discovered or God knows," he babbled, practically embracing Clarey in a fervency of relief. "I was afraid—"

"Come, come, Colonel," Clarey interrupted, striding past him, "you know how inefficient Damorlant transport is, and I had to make two chain connections."

"Of course," the colonel said, wiping the perspiration off his forehead. "Of course. And you must be dead tired. Sit down; let me take your cloak—"

"How about the servants?" Clarey asked.

"This is their weekend off." Blynn pulled himself together. "Really, my dear fellow, I've been in this business longer than you. I know what precautions to take."

"Never can be too careful."

"I see you've got yourself another cloak," the colonel said as he hung it in the guest snap. "Very handsome. I've never seen one like it."

"Yes. As a matter of fact, several people on the chains wanted to know where I'd got it."

"Where *did* you get it?" asked Blynn, feeling the material. "Might go well as an export."

"Afraid it couldn't be exported. It's a custom job, you see. Handwoven, hand-decorated. It was a birthday present."

The colonel stared at him.

"Well," Clarey said, "if you didn't expect me to get birthday presents, you shouldn't have put a birth date on my identity papers. My boss baked me a melxhane—"

"Your boss?"

"The relationship between employer and employee is much different from the way it is on Earth," Clarey explained. Reaching over, he flipped the switch on the recorder and repeated the statement, adding, "Embelsira is kind, considerate, helpful; she can't do enough for me." He put his mouth close to the mechanism. "Be sure to tell MacFingal that."

"Now, now," the colonel said, turning the switch off. He pushed a small tea wagon over to Clarey. "You must be starving. Have some sandwiches and coffee. I'm sure you'll be glad to taste good Earth food again."

"Yes, indeed," Clarey said, trying not to make a face. "Er—shouldn't we start recording while everything's fresh in my mind?"

"Might as well," the colonel said, flipping the switch again. "Pity we don't have a probe here. Would save so much time. But, of course, it's an expensive installation. All right, Clarey, over to you."

CLAREY choked on a mouthful of sandwich and hesitated. "Begin with your very first impressions," the colonel urged.

"Well, the archives—the library—was in a real mess. Took me over two weeks to get it in even roughly decent shape. Three different systems of classification and, added to that—"

"Not so much the library, old chap. Leave the technical stuff for later. What I meant was your first impressions of the natives... Is something wrong with the coffee? And you've hardly touched your sandwich. Maybe you'd like another kind. I have several varieties here—ham and cheese and—"

"Oh, no," Clarey protested. "The one I have is fine. It's just that I'm—well, to tell you the truth," he confessed, "I've grown accustomed to Damorlant food."

"Don't see how you could," the colonel said. "Nauseating stuff—to my way of thinking," he added politely. He opened a sandwich and inspected the filling.

"You've only eaten at public places. Even the better restaurants don't put themselves out for Earthmen, say they have no palates, I guess the word would be. But you ought to taste my landlady's cooking..."

"All this is being taped, you know. They'll have to listen to every word on Earth."

"If only I could convey the true picture through words. Her ragouts are rhapsodies, her soufflés symphonies—I'm using rough Terrestrial equivalents, of course—"

"The cuisine comes later, please. Over-all impressions first."

"Well," Clarey began again, "at first I was a bit surprised that you'd stuck me in a quarter-credit place like Katund. Naturally in a village the people'd be more backward than in the cities, so you'd have a poorer idea of how they were developing. Then I realized that you couldn't help putting me there, that you probably couldn't write a letter good enough to get me a job in any of the big centers. Embelsira said she was surprised to find me so much more literate than she would have expected from the letter."

The colonel sat erect huffily. "I've never pretended to be a philologist. And, anyway, Damorlan isn't like Earth. Here the heartbeat of the planet is in its villages."

"Earth hasn't any villages, so the comparison doesn't apply." Clarey cleared his throat. "Don't you have anything to drink except coffee?"

"Tea?"

"That would be better. Do you know the Katundi have a special variety of tea, or something very much like it, which is—"

"Tell me what they think of Earthmen," the colonel interrupted desperately.

"Not much. What I mean is, nobody in Katund's actually had any contact with them, though they've heard of them, of course. Every now and then there's a little article in the Dordonec Bulletin from their Barshwat correspondent, and sometimes, if there isn't any real news, he gives a couple of inches to the Earthmen."

"Exactly how do they regard us?" the colonel asked as he spooned tea into the pot. "Demigods? Superior beings? Are they in great awe of us?"

"They regard us as visitors from another planet," Clarey said. "They don't realize from quite how far away we hail, think it's only a matter of a solar system or two, but they've got the general idea. Don't forget, they may not be a mechanical people, but they do have some idea of astronomy. They're not illiterate clods."

"What do they think of our spaceships? Great floating platforms, something like that?"

SIGHING deeply, Clarey said, "They think our spaceships are massive cars or buses that fly through the sky without tracks. And they think it's silly, our having machines to fly in the sky and none to go on the ground. There's an old Dordonec proverb: 'One must run before one must fly.' Originally applied to birds, but—"

"But what else do they think about us?"

Clarey was hurt. "That's what I was getting to, if you'll only give me time. After all, I've been speaking Vangtort for six months and it's a little hard to go back to Terran and organize my thoughts at the same time."

"Terribly sorry," the colonel apologized, handing him a cup of tea. "Carry on."

"Thank you. They say if you—if we—are so smart, why do we use hax or the chains like anybody else? They think somebody else must have given us the starships, or else we stole them. That's mostly Piq's idea; he's the village lawyer and, of course, lawyers are apt to think in terms like that."

"Um," the colonel said. "We didn't think it would be a good idea to introduce ground cars. Upset their traffic and cause dissatisfied yearnings."

"They're satisfied with their hax carts. They're not in any hurry to get anywhere. But Katund's a village. Attitudes may be different in the cities."

"You stick with your village, old chap. If you feel a wild urge for city life, you can always take a weekend trip to Zrig. Stay at the Zrig Grasht; it's the only decent inn. By the way, you spoke of a landlady. Do you mean at the inn?"

No, Clarey told him, at first he had put up at the inn, but he found the place noisy, the cooking poor, and the pallet covers dirty. Besides, Hanxi had kept importuning him to go on visits to a nearby township where he promised him a good time.

"I was wondering, though," Clarey finished, "if it would be possible for an Earthman and a Damorlant to—er—have a good time together."

"Been wondering myself," the colonel said eagerly. "I didn't dare ask on my own behalf, but it's your job, isn't it? I'll check back with the X-T boys on Earth. Go on with your story."

AS A RESIDENT of the inn, Clarey told Colonel Blynn, he'd found that he was expected to join the men in the bar parlor every evening, where they'd drink and exchange appropriate stories. But he'd choked on the squfur and was insufficiently familiar with the local mores to be able to appreciate the stories, let alone tell any. He'd concentrated on smiling and agreeing with whatever anybody said, with the result that the others began to agree with Piq that he was a bit cracked. "They were, for the most part, polite enough to me, but I could sense the gulf. I was a stranger, a city man, and probably a bit of a lunatic."

A few of the younger ones hadn't even been polite. "They used to insult me obliquely," Clarey went on, "and whisper things I only half-heard. I pretended I didn't hear at all. I stood them drinks and told them what a lovely place Katund was, so much cleaner and prettier and friendlier than the city. That just seemed to confirm their impression that I was an idiot."

He stopped, took a sip of tea, and continued, "The females' were friendly enough, though. Every time they came into the library they'd always stop for a chat. And they were very hospitable—invited me to outdoor luncheons, temple gatherings, things like that. Embelsira—she's the chief librarian—got quite annoyed because she said they made so much noise when they all gathered round my desk."

He paused and blushed. "I have an idea that—well, the ladies don't find me unattractive. I mean they're not really ladies. That is, they're perfect ladies; they're just not women."

"I'm not a bit surprised," the colonel nodded sagely. "Very well-set-up young fellow for a native—only natural they should take a liking to you. And only natural the men shouldn't."

Clarey gave an embarrassed grin. "One evening I was sitting in the bar-parlor, talking to Kuqal and Gazmor, two of the older men. And then Mundes came in; he's the town muscle boy. You know the type—one in every tri-di series. He was rather unpleasant. I pretended to think he was joking. I've learned to laugh like one of them. Listen." He gave a creditable imitation of an agonized turshi.

THE colonel shuddered. "I'm sure if anything would convince the chaps back on Earth that the Damorlanti aren't human, that would do it. What then?"

"Finally he made a remark impugning the virility of librarians that I simply could not ignore, so I emptied my mug of squfur in his face."

"Stout fellow!"

"I knew he'd attack me and probably beat me up, but I thought that perhaps if I put up a show of courage they'd respect me. There was something like that in *Sentries of the Sky* a year or so ago—but of course you'd have missed that episode; you were up here. Anyhow, as I expected, he hit me. And then I hit him..." He smiled reminiscently into his cup of tea.

"And then?"

"I beat him," Clarey said simply. "I still can't figure out how I did it. I think it must be because my muscles are heavier-gravity type." He smiled again. "And I beat him good. He couldn't dance at the temple for weeks."

The colonel's jaw dropped. "He's a temple dancer?"

"Chief temple dancer. I was a little worried about that, because I didn't want to get in bad theologically. So I went to the priest and apologized for any inconvenience I might have caused. He said not to worry; Mundes had had it coming to him for a long time and his one regret was that he hadn't been there to see it. Then we touched toes and he said he liked to see a young fellow with brawn who also took an interest in cultural pursuits like reading. He trusted I'd have a beneficial effect on the youth of the village. And then he asked me to fill in for Mundes as chief temple dancer until he—ah—recovered. It's a great honor, you know," he said sharply, as the colonel seemed more moved to mirth than awe. "But I've never been much of a dancing man and that's what I told him."

"Very well done," the colonel said approvingly. "But you still haven't explained where you got lodgings and a landlady."

"She's Embelsira's mother. I was invited over for dinner from time to time... It's a local custom," he explained as Blynn's eyebrows went up. "So, when Embelsira told me her mother happened to have a compartment to let with meals included, I jumped at it. Blynn, you really ought to taste those pastries of hers."

The colonel managed to divert him onto some of the other aspects of Katundut life. When he'd finished taping everything he had to say, the colonel gave him a list of artifacts and small-sized flora and fauna the specialists on Earth wanted him to collect for his next trip, providing he could do so without arousing attention or violating taboos.

They shook hands. "Clarey," the colonel said, "you've done splendidly. Earth will be proud of you. And you might bring along one or two of those pastries, by the way."

WHEN Clarey got back to Katund, Embelsira and her mother gave a little welcome home party for him. "Nothing elaborate," the widow said. "Just a few neighbors and friends, some simple refreshments."

The tiny residential dome was packed with people; the refreshments, Clarey thought, as he munched industriously; were magnificent. But then he'd been forced to live on Earth food for weekend, so he was no judge.

After they'd finished eating, the young people folded the furniture, and, while one of the boys played upon a curious instrument that was string and percussion and brass all at once, the others danced.

Clarey made no attempt to participate. In his early youth, he'd flopped at the Earth hops—and the Damorlanti had a distinctly more Dionysian culture than his home world. He stood and watched them leaping and twirling. When they'd dropped, temporarily exhausted, he made his way over to the musician, whom he recognized as one of Piq's numerous grandsons; this one was Rini, he thought.

"Is that difficult to learn?" he asked, touching the instrument.

"The ulerin is extremely difficult," the boy said importantly. "It takes years and years of practice. And you've got to have the touch to begin with. Not many do. All our family have the touch, my brother Irik most of all. He's in Barshwat, studying to be a famous musician."

Clarey looked at the ulerin with unmistakable wistfulness.

"Care to try it?" the boy asked. "But, mind, you have to pay for any bladders you burst."

"I shall be very careful," Clarey said, taking the instrument reverently in his hands. He had never touched a musical instrument before—an Earth instrument would have been no less unfamiliar, no more wonderful. Gently he began to pluck and bang and blow, in imitation of the way the boy had done, and, though the sounds that came out didn't have the same smoothness, still they didn't fall harshly on his ears. The others stopped talking and listened; it would have been difficult for them to do otherwise, as he was unable to find the muting device.

"Sounds like the death wail of a hix," Piq sibilated, but he added grudgingly, "Foreigner or not, I have to say this for him—he's got the touch."

"Yes, he's got the touch," others agreed. "You always can tell."

Rini smiled at Clarey. "I believe you do. I'll teach you to play, if you like."

"I would, very much." Clarey was about to offer to pay for the lessons; then he remembered that, though this would have been the right thing on Earth, it would be wrong on Damorlan. "If it is not too much trouble," he finished.

"It's the kind of trouble I like." The boy twisted his nose at Clarey. "Sometime you can hide the reserved books for me."

AFTER the guests had gone, Clarey insisted on helping the women with the putting away. "Well, as long as Embelsira has a pair of brawny arms to help her," the widow yawned, "I might as well be getting along to my pallet. I seem to get more and more tired these days—old age, I expect. One day I'll be so tired I'll never wake up and Embelsira'll be alone and what'll she do, poor thing? Who can live on a librarian's salary? Now, on two librarians' salaries—"

"Mother," Embelsira interrupted furiously, "you go to bed!"

She did, hurriedly.

"Don't worry, Embelsira," Clarey said. "She will be weaving away for decades yet. Everybody says she's the best weaver in the district," he added, to change the subject.

"Yes," Embelsira said as they gathered all the oddments the guests had left. "She's been offered a lot of money to go work in Zrig. But she won't leave Katund; she was born here, and so were her parents."

"I do not blame her for wanting to stay," he said. "It's a very—homelike place."

She sighed. "To us it is, but I don't suppose someone who's city born and bred would feel the same way. I know you won't let yourself stay buried here forever, and what will I—what will Mother and I ever do without you?"

"It is—very kind of you to say so," he replied. "I am honored."

The girl—she was still young enough to be called a girl, though no longer in her first youth—looked up at him. Blue eyes could be pleasing in their way. "Why are you always so stiff, so cold?"

"I am not cold," he said honestly. "I am—afraid."

"There is nothing to be afraid of. You're safe, among friends, no matter what you may have done back where you came from."

"But I have done nothing back there," he said. "Nothing at all. Perhaps that is the trouble with me."

She looked up at him and then away. "Then isn't it about time you started to do something?"

THE NEXT time he went to Barshwat he took a lot of luggage with him, because, besides the artifacts and the flora and fauna, he brought cold pastries for the colonel. The colonel ate one in silence, then said, "Try to get the recipe."

"By the way," said Clarey, "the X-T boys made a few mistakes. The bugg isn't an insect; it's a bird. And the lule isn't a bird; it's a flower. And the paparun isn't a flower; it's an insect."

"Oh, well, I guess they'll be able to straighten that out," the colonel said, licking crumbs from his thick fingers. "We do our jobs and they do theirs." He reached for another pastry.

"Take good care of the bugg," Clarey said. "He likes his morning seed mixed with milk; his evening seed with wine. His name is Mirti. He's very tame and affectionate. I said I was bringing him to my aunt..." He paused. "You are going to take him back alive, aren't you? You'd get so much more information that way."

"Wouldn't dream of hurting a hair—a feather—no, it is a hair, isn't it?—of the little fellow's head."

Clarey looked out of the window at the purple night sky. Then he turned back to the colonel. "I've been taking music lessons," he said defiantly.

"Fine. Every man should have a hobby."

"But I've no music license."

"Come now, Clarey. You still don't seem to realize you're on Damorlan, not Earth. Not a blooded intelligence man yet. There aren't any guilds on Damorlan, so enjoy yourself."

"Speaking of that, did you find out about—er—Earthmen and—"

"Yes, I'd meant to drop you a note, but it seemed rather odd information for your aunt to be giving you. It's absolutely all right, old chap. Go ahead, have your bit of fun."

Clarey was unreasonably annoyed. "I wasn't thinking of what you're thinking. I mean—well, Katund is a village and the native morality is very strict in these matters."

"Afraid I don't quite follow you."

Clarey bit his finger. "Well," he finally admitted, "the truth of the matter is I'd like to get married."

The colonel was extremely surprised. "A legal arrangement? Is it absolutely necessary? How about the females that the innkeeper's so anxious to have you—ah—meet?"

CLAREY didn't know how to explain. "Their standards of cleanliness…" he began, and stopped. Then he started again: "I suppose I'd like a permanent companion."

"I don't suppose there's any real reason why you shouldn't enter into a legal liaison while you're here," said the colonel. "After all, it isn't as if the two races could interbreed. That could be decidedly awkward. Who's the lucky little lady?"

"My landlady's daughter," Clarey said.

"Your boss, eh? Flying high, aren't you, old chap?" His massive hand descended on Clarey's shoulder. Then he grew serious. "Can she cook like her mother?"

"Even better."

"My boy," the colonel said solemnly, "you have my unqualified blessing. And when I ask you to save me a piece of the wedding cake, I ask from the heart."

165

So, when Clarey went back to Katund, he asked Embelsira to marry him and she accepted. The whole village turned out for the wedding. Clarey managed to take some vocpix of the ceremonies for the X-Ts with a finger unit. I ought to get a handsome wedding present for this, he thought.

And, to his surprise, on the wedding day, an elaborate jewel-studded toilet service did arrive from Barshwat— with the affectionate regards of his aunt, who was too ill to travel. They tie up everything, he thought, but he knew it was a little more than simply remembering to pick up a loose end. The toilet set was vulgar, ostentatious, hideous—obviously selected with loving care and Terrestrial taste.

Everybody in Katund and a lot of people from the surrounding country came to look at it. It seemed to establish his eligibility beyond a doubt. "Never thought 'Belsira'd do it, and at her age, too," Piq was heard to comment. "But it looks like she really got herself a catch. What's a little weakness in the dome-top when there's money, too?"

CHAPTER THREE

THE FIRST three years of Clarey's marriage were happy ones. He and Embelsira got on very nicely together and, since he was fond of her mother, he didn't mind her constant presence too much. Once a week he took a ulerin lesson from Rini. He practiced assiduously and made progress that he himself could see was sensational. He did wish that Rini would accept money; it would have been so much less of a nuisance than replacing the music books the boy stole from the library, but he couldn't expect local customs to coincide with his own. The money, of course, didn't matter; he still wasn't living up to his allowance, although he was beginning to spread himself on elaborate custom-made cloaks and tunics. On Earth he had dressed soberly, according to his status, but here he felt entitled to cut a dash.

At the colonel's request, on his next trip to Barshwat he brought his ulerin and taped some native melodies. "I like 'em," the colonel said, nodding his head emphatically. "Catchy, very catchy. Hope the X-Ts appreciate them; they don't usually like music if it sounds at all human." And, catching the look on Clarey's face, "Well, you know what I mean. To them, if a tune can be hummed, it isn't authentic."

News of Clarey's skill on the ulerin spread through the countryside. When he played in the temple concerts, people sometimes came from as far away as Zrig to hear him. Clarey was a little disturbed about this, because he didn't subscribe to the local faith. But the high priest said,

"My son, music knows no religious boundaries. Besides, when you play, we always get three times as much in the collection nets."

At the time Clarey got word from Barshwat that General Spano and the staff ship were expected shortly, he had risen to the post of chief librarian. Embelsira had retired to keep dome and wait for the young ones who would, of course, never come. Clarey had hired a hixhead of an assistant from Zrig to assist him; he saw now why the village had originally been grateful to get even a foreigner of doubtful background for the job.

"I'm going to have to stay at least a week with Aunt Askush this time," he told his wife. "Legal matters. I think she's drawing up a will or some such," he added, hoping that this would keep Embelsira happy and convinced.

Maybe it worked too well. "But why can't I come with you? I've always wanted so much to meet her."

"I keep telling you her illness is a disfiguring one; she won't meet strangers. And don't say you're not a stranger—you'd understand, but she's the one who wouldn't. Please don't nag me, Belsir."

"Sometimes I think you're a stranger, Balt," Embelsira declared emotionally.

"Yes, dear, I'm a stranger, anything you say, but let me get packed." He started folding a robe crookedly, hoping it would distract her into taking over the job.

But she leaned against the lintel, staring at him. "Balt, sometimes I wonder if you really have an aunt."

The only thing he allowed himself to do was put down the robe he was holding. "Do you think I send expensive toilet sets to myself? You must think Piq's right—I'm just plain crazy."

"Piq doesn't think you're crazy anymore. He and the other old ones say you have a woman in Barshwat. But I don't believe that."

"Maybe I do, Embelsira. A man's a man, even if he is a librarian."

"I know it isn't true. I think it's...something else entirely. You're so strange sometimes, Balt. How could somebody who comes only from the other side of the same world be so strange?"

HE forced a grin. "Suddenly you've become very cosmic. What do you know of our—of the world? It's a big place. And nobody else in Katund seems to be so impressed by my strangeness; they think a foreigner's entitled to his queer ways."

"Nobody in Katund knows I you as well as I do. And I've I seen foreigners before. They're not different in the way you are." She looked intently at him. "It's not a shameful kind of strangeness, just a...strange kind of strangeness. Fascinating in its way—I don't want you to think I just married the first stranger who came along..."

"I'm sure you had many offers, dear. Come, help me fold this cloak or I'll never make the bus."

"You know what I'm reminded of?" she said, coming forward and taking the cloak. "Of the old tale about the lovely village maiden who marries the handsome stranger and promises she'll never look into his eyes. And then one day she forgets and looks into his eyes and sees—"

"What does she see?"

"The worst thing of all, the greatest horror. She sees nothing. She sees emptiness."

He laughed. "The moral's clear. She shouldn't have looked into his eyes."

"But how can you help looking into the eyes of the man you love? Maybe that's the moral—that it was an impossible task he set her."

"In those tales it's always the man's fault, isn't it? Not much doubt who made them up. Now, Belsir, please, I've got to finish packing. It'll be just my luck to have today be the day the bus to Zrig's on time."

"A couple of weeks ago I was in Zrig shopping and I saw an Earthman," she said, folding his cloak into the kit. "The way he walked, the way he moved, reminded me a little of you."

It was a long moment before he could speak. "Do I look to you like a dark-faced, dark-haired, brown-eyed—"

"I didn't say you *were* an Earthman. But if Earthmen can travel through the sky, they might be able to do other things, too; maybe even change the way a man looks."

He snapped the kit-fastener. "If you really believe that, you should be careful. Creatures as clever as that might be able to pluck your words from my brain."

"What if they did? I'm not ashamed. Or afraid, either."

He reached out and patted her arm. Maybe she wasn't afraid, but he was. For her. And for the people of Damorlan. If there was a deep-probe on the staff ship... If only something could happen to him, so he could never reach Barshwat... Spano wouldn't know. He might guess, but he wouldn't know. He'd have to start all over again and maybe things would turn out better next time.

GENERAL SPANO and his secretary were waiting in Blynn's office. Clarey stretched out his foot in greeting, then recollected himself and reached out his hand. "You see, sir," he said with a too-hearty laugh, "I'm really living my part."

Spano beamed. "Damorlan certainly seems to agree with you, my boy. You look positively blooming. Doesn't he, Han?"

She nodded grave agreement.

The general sniffed. "What's that you two are smoking?"

"Marac leaves," Clarey said. "A native product. Care to try one?" He extended his pouch to Spano.

"Don't mind if I do," the general said, taking a roll. "Which part do you light? And why don't you offer one to Secretary Vollard?"

"Oh, sorry; I didn't think of it. The women here don't use it. Care to try one, Secretary?" As she took a roll, she looked at him searchingly. She was still beautiful in an Amazonian way, but he preferred Embelsira's way. He could never imagine Han Vollard warm and tender.

"Well, Clarey," Spano said, "you seem to be doing a splendid job. I've been absolutely enthralled by your reports." He settled himself behind Blynn's desk. "Pity the information's top secret. It could make a fortune on the tri-dis."

Clarey bowed.

"And those musictapes you sent back created quite a stir. We've brought along some superior equipment. The rig here is good enough for routine work, but we need better fidelity for this. And it would be appreciated if the colonel didn't beat time with his foot while you played— no offense, Blynn."

He turned back to Clarey. "Do you think you can pick up some of those what-do-you-call-'ems—ulerins—for us, too, or is there a taboo of some kind?"

"Not ulerins," Clarey corrected, "uleran. And you can walk up to any marketplace and get as many as you like—providing you have the cash, of course."

"I *told* you the job had musical overtones. I'll bet that makes up for some of the discomforts and privations."

"It's not too uncomfortable."

"There speaks a true patriot," Spano approved.

Han measured Clarey with her eyes. "You're quiet, Secretary," he said nervously. "You used to talk a lot more."

Blynn stared at him. She smiled. "You're the one who has things to tell now, Clarey."

"And show," the general said, almost licking his lips. "Every one of your tapes made my mouth fairly water. I trust you brought an ample and varied supply of those delicacies."

Clarey's smile was unforced this time. "I got your message and I brought along a large hamperful, but it'll be hard to make the people back home keep thinking my aunt's an invalid if she eats like a team of hax. My wife baked some pastries that I especially recommend to your attention."

"I think we ought to get business over before we start on refreshments," Han suggested.

"Yes," Spano agreed reluctantly. "I suppose you had better be deep-probed first, Clarey... Not even one taste beforehand, Han...? Well, I suppose not."

Clarey tensed. "You've got a probe on the ship?" he asked, as if the possibility had never occurred to him.

"That's right," Han Vollard said. "It's an up-to-date model. The whole thing'll take you less than an hour, and we'll have the information collated by morning."

"I—I would prefer not to be deep-probed. You never can tell: it might upset all the conditioning I've received here; it—"

"Let us worry about that, Clarey," she said.

HE DIDN'T sleep that night. He sat looking out of the window, knowing there was nothing he could do. Embelsira was in danger—her people were in danger and he couldn't lift a finger to save them.

When he came down to breakfast, he saw that the reports had been collated and read. "So your wife suspects, does she?" the general asked. "Shrewd little creature. You must have picked one of the more intelligent ones."

Clarey struggled on the pin. "Wives often have strange fancies about their husbands. You mustn't take it too seriously."

"How often have you been married, Clarey?" Han asked. "Or even linked in liaison? How many married people did you know well back on Earth?"

There was no need to answer; she knew all the answers.

"I think Clarey did a rattling good job," Blynn said stoutly. "It wasn't his fault that she suspects."

"Of course not," the general agreed. "Feminine intuition isn't restricted to human females. In fact, in some female ilfs it's even stronger than in humans. The precognitive faculties in the grua, for example—"

"What are you going to do?" Clarey interrupted bluntly.

Han Vollard answered him: "Nothing yet. You've got us a lot of information, but it's not enough. You'll have to keep on as you are for another three years or so."

It was all Clarey could do to keep from trembling visibly with relief.

"It doesn't even matter too much that one of the natives suspects," Han went on, "as long as she doesn't definitely know."

"She doesn't," Clarey said, "and she won't. And she won't tell anybody; she'd be afraid for me." But he wasn't all that sure. The Damorlanti didn't hate Earthmen and they didn't fear them, and so Embelsira wouldn't think it was a shameful thing to be. He was glad he'd already been deep-probed. At least this thought would be safe for three years or so.

"At any rate, they don't seem antagonistic toward Earthmen," the general said, almost as if he'd read part of Clarey's mind. "I think that's nice."

Han Vollard looked at him. "It's not their attitude toward us that matters. They couldn't do anything if they tried. It's what they are that matters, what they will be that matters even more."

"I take back what I said before," Clarey flared. "You talk too damn much."

There was a chilling silence.

"Nerves," said Blynn nervously. "Every agent lets go when he's back among his own kind. Nothing but release of tension."

SEVERAL days later the staff ship was ready to go back to Earth. "Don't forget to tell your wife how much I enjoyed the pies," Spano said; then, "Oh, I was forgetting; you could hardly do that. But do see if you can work out something with the dehydro-freeze. I'd hate to have to wait three years before tasting them again. You can keep your marac rolls, though; I'll take my smoke-sticks."

"Try not to get any more involved, Clarey," Han Vollard said as they stood outside the airlock. "Maybe you ought to move on—to a city, perhaps, another country—"

"When I want your advice, I'll ask for it," he snapped.

After they'd gone, Blynn turned on him. "Man, you must be out of your mind, talking to Secretary Vollard like that."

"Why does she have to keep meddling? It's none of her business—"

"None of her business? Secretary of the Space Service, and you say it's none of her business?"

Clarey blinked. "I thought she was Spano's secretary."

Blynn laughed until the tears dampened his dark cheeks. "Spano's only Head of Intelligence. She's his Mistress."

"Of course—*mistress*, feminine of *master*. I should have realized that before." Then Clarey laughed, too. "I'm a real all-round alien. I can't even understand my own language."

On the way back home he couldn't help thinking that Han Vollard might be right. It could be the best thing for him to disappear now; the best thing for himself, the best thing for Embelsira. He could pretend to desert her— better yet, Blynn could fake some kind of accident, so her feelings wouldn't be hurt. A pension of some kind would be arranged. She could marry again, have the children she wanted so much. If he waited the full ten years, she might never be able to have them. He had no idea at what age Damorlant females ceased to be fertile.

But she wasn't just a Damorlant female—she was his wife. He didn't want to leave her. Maybe he never would have to. Hadn't Spano said that when his term was over he could pick his planet? He would pick Damorlan.

WHEN Clarey came home from Barshwat, Embelsira said nothing more about her suspicions, but greeted him affectionately and prepared a special supper for him. Afterward, he wondered if making love to an Earth girl could be as pleasant. He wondered how it would be to make love to Han Vollard.

The days passed and he forgot about Han Vollard. After much persuasion, he agreed to give a series of concerts at Zrig, but only on condition that Rini played with him and had one solo each performance. He was embarrassed at having so far outstripped his teacher, but Rini seemed unperturbed.

"My technique's still better than yours will ever be," he said. "It's this new style of yours that gets 'em. I understand it's spreading; it's reached as far as Barshwat. You should see the angry letters Irik writes about it," Rini chuckled. "And he hasn't the least idea it started right here in his own home village that he's always sneered at for being so backward."

Clarey smiled and clapped the boy on the neck. If it made Rini feel better to think Clarey had a new style rather than that Clarey played better than he did, Clarey had no objection.

Clarey was offered the post of head librarian at Zrig, but Embelsira didn't want to leave Katund; and, when he thought about it, he really didn't want to either. So he refused the job and didn't bother mentioning the matter to Headquarters.

As he grew more sure of himself and his position, he allowed his wealth to show. He and Embelsira moved into a larger dome. Instead of sending to Zrig or even Barshwat for the furnishings, they hired local talent. Tavan, the carpenter, made them some exquisite blackwood pieces inlaid with opalescent stone that everyone said was the equal of anything in Barshwat. A talented nephew of Hanxi's painted glowing murals; Embelsira's mother wove rugs and draperies in muted water-tones. The dome became the district showplace. Clarey realized he now had a position to keep up, but sometimes it annoyed him when perfect strangers asked to see the place.

He was invited to run against Malesor as headman but declined. He didn't want to be brought into undue prominence. Trouble was, as he became popular, he also aroused animosity. There were the girls who felt he should have married them instead of Embelsira, and their mothers and subsequent husbands. A lot of people resented Clarey because they felt he should have decorated his house differently, dressed differently, spent his money differently.

A man can live ignored by everyone, he discovered, but he can't be liked by some without finding himself disliked by others.

MATTERS came to a head in his fourth spring there. He thought of it as spring, although on Damorlan the seasons had no separate identities; they blended into one another, without its ever being very hot or very cold, very rainy or very dry. The reason he called this time of the year spring was that it seemed closest to perfection.

It was less perfect that year. Because it was then that Rini's brother Irik came back from Barshwat, after a six years' absence. He was very much the city man, far more so than anyone Clarey had seen in Barshwat itself. His tunics were shorter than his fellow villagers, and his cloaks iridesced restlessly from one vivid color to another. He wore a great deal of jewelry and perfume, neither of the best quality, and the toes of his boots were divided.

Clarey described this in detail to Embelsira the night Irik put in his first appearance at the Furbush. "You should have seen the little horror."

"That's the way city men dress," Embelsira told him. "It's fashionable."

"But, dear, I've been to Barshwat."

"You don't have an eye for clothes. You never notice when I put on anything new. And I think it's unfair to take a dislike to Irik just because you don't care for the way he dresses."

"It's more than that, Belsira." And yet how could he explain to her what he couldn't quite understand himself, that Irik was vain, stupid, hostile; hence, dangerous?

"I swear to you, Balt," Embelsira said demurely, "that whatever there was between me and Irik, it all ended six years ago."

Clarey gave a start and then held back a smile. "I believe you, dear," And he kissed her nose.

IRIK held forth in the Furbush every evening of his stay in Katund. He had grievances and he aired them generously. He hated everything—the government, taxes, modern music, and Earthmen, whom he seemed to consider in some way responsible for the modern music, or at least its popularization. "Barbarians—slept completely through my concerts."

"But people are always falling asleep during concerts, Irik," Malesor pointed out reasonably. "And how could you expect barbarians to appreciate good music? What do you care for Earthmen's opinions as long as your own people like your music?"

Irik hesitated. "But the Earthmen have taken up the new kind of music; they stay awake during that. And—a lot of people seem to think that whatever's strange is good, so whatever the Earthmen like eventually becomes fashionable."

Hanxi wiggled his ears. "Fashions change. Well, who's ready to have his mug refilled?"

"But the Earthmen will keep on setting the fashions," Irik snarled. "Many people think the Earthmen know everything, just because they're aloof and have sky cars."

"Well," Malesor said, "the sky cars certainly prove they know something we don't. Better stick to your music, boy."

The smoky little bar-parlor resounded with laughter and Irik's face turned a nasty red. "They don't know anything about music and they don't know everything about machinery. We might surprise them yet. A friend of mine knows Guhak, the fellow who invented that new brake for the track car a few years ago."

"We know about that brake," Piq observed. "It stops a car so good, the chains are twice as late nowadays as they used to be, and you couldn't strictly say they were ever on time."

Everybody laughed again. Irik quivered with anger. "Guhak has invented a car that doesn't need to go on tracks. It can run whenever it wants wherever it wants. And one car will be able to go faster than three hax teams."

"That I'll believe when I've ridden on it," Kuqal grinned. "Even the chains aren't that fast." The others bit their thumbs and nodded—except Clarey, who was rigidly keeping out of the conversation. He forced squfur down his tightening throat and said nothing.

"You're backward clods," Irik raged. "If the Earthmen can have cars that go through the sky without tracks why shouldn't we have cars that run on the ground the same way? Have we tried?"

"Doesn't seem to me it's worth the effort," Malesor said. "Our cars can get us where we're going as fast as we need to go already, why bother?"

"Whatever an Earthman can do, we can do better. Soon Guhak will get his ground cars on the road. After that, it'll only be a short step to cars that go in the sky. Then we'll find out where the Earthmen come from and why they're here. We'll be as powerful as they are. We'll get rid of them and their rotten music."

The bar-parlor was silent, except for the clink as Clarey put his mug on the table. If he held it an instant longer, he was afraid he would spill it. One or two of the men looked at him uneasily out of the corners of their eyes. Malesor spoke: "In the first place, you don't know how powerful Earthmen are. In the second place, who wants to be powerful, anyway? The Earthmen haven't done us any harm and they're a good thing for the economy. My cousin in Zrig tells me one of 'em come into his store a coupla months ago and bought out his whole stock, every bolt of cloth. Paid twice what it was worth, too. Live and let live, I say."

The others murmured restlessly.

"If there are ways of doing things better," Rini suggested, "why shouldn't we have them, too?" His eyes darted quickly toward Clarey's and then as quickly away.

Irik turned his head and looked directly at Clarey for the first time. "You're silent, stranger. What do *you* think of the Earthmen?"

CLAREY picked up his drink, finished the squfur and set the mug back down on the table. "I don't know much about Earthmen. An ugly-looking lot, true, but there doesn't seem to be any harm in them. Of course, living in Barshwat, you probably know a lot more about them than I do."

"I doubt that," Irik said. "You have an aunt in Barshwat."

Clarey allowed himself to look surprised before he said courteously, "I'm glad you find me and my family so interesting. Yes, it so happens I do have an aunt there, but she's rather advanced in years and doesn't enjoy hanging around the starship field the way the children do."

Irik's face darkened. "What is your aunt's name?"

This time everyone looked surprised. The question itself was not too out-of-the-way, but his tone decidedly was.

"She's a great-grandmother," Clarey said. "She would be too old for you. And I assure you it's difficult to part her from her money. I've tried."

Everybody laughed. Irik was furious. "I understand that your aunt lives very close to Earth Headquarters."

Somebody must have followed him on one or more of his trips to Barshwat, Clarey realized. "If the Earthmen chose to establish themselves in the best residential section of Barshwat, near the great inland sea, then probably my aunt does live near them. She's not the type to leave a comfortable dome with a beautiful view of the sea and the mountains simply because foreigners move into the neighborhood."

"Perhaps she has more than neighborhood in common with Earthmen."

The room was suddenly very quiet again.

"She does sometimes go to sleep at concerts," Clarey conceded.

Irik opened his mouth. Malesor held up a hand. "Before you say anything more against the Earthmen, Irik," he advised, "you oughta find out more about them. Their cars move faster and higher than ours. Maybe their catapults do, too."

No one looked at Clarey. Malesor had averted a showdown, he knew, but this was the beginning of the end. And he had a suspicion who was responsible—innocently perhaps, perhaps not. Love does not always imply trust. And when he told Embelsira what had happened in the Furbush, she, too, couldn't meet his eye. "That Irik," she said, "I never liked him."

"I wonder how he knows so much about me."

"Rini writes him very often," she babbled. "He must have told him you were responsible for the new music. That would make him hate you. Rini likes to irritate Irik, because he's always been jealous of him. But the whole thing's silly. How could you possibly make over the world's music, even if you were—" Her voice ran down.

"An Earthman?" he finished coldly. "I suppose you went around telling everybody your suspicions, and Rini wrote that to Irik, too?"

"I DIDN'T tell anybody," she protested indignantly. "Not a soul." She met his eye. "Except Mother, of course."

"Your mother? You might as well have published it in the District Bulletin!"

"You have no right to speak of Mother like that, even if it's true!" Embelsira began to sob. "I had to tell her, Balt—she kept asking why there weren't any young ones."

"You could've told her to mind her own business," he snapped, before he could catch himself. Five years, and he still made slips. It was her business. On Damorlan, it was a woman's duty; not only to have children but to see that her children had children and their children had children.

He made himself look grave and self-reproachful. "I have a confession to make, Belsir. I should have told you when I married you, I can't have children."

"I never heard of such a thing. Everybody has children—unless they're not married, of course," she added primly.

"It's an affliction sent by the gods."

"The gods would never do anything like that," she declared confidently.

How primitive she is, he thought, and then, angrily, how provincial *I* am. He had never stopped to think about it, but he knew of no married couple who had not at least one offspring; he and Embelsira were the only ones. It hadn't occurred to the X-T specialists that a species whose biological assets were roughly the same might have different handicaps. Apparently there was no such thing as sterility on Damorlan.

"Are you really an Earthman, then, Balt?" she asked timidly.

She had spread the news around, ruined him, ruined the work Earth had been doing, perhaps ruined even more than that—and she hadn't even been sure to begin with. But it was too late for recriminations. He had to salvage what little he could—time, maybe; that was all.

"Are you going to tell?" he asked.

She hesitated. "Do you swear you don't mean my people any harm?"

"I swear," he said.

"Then I swear not to tell," she said.

He kissed her. After all, he thought, it isn't a lie. I don't mean her people any harm. Besides, sooner or later, her mother will get it out of her, so she won't be keeping her part of the bargain.

THE NEXT time he went to Barshwat he knew he would be followed. He tried to shake the follower or followers off, but he couldn't be sure he'd succeeded.

He found the colonel looking out of the window with an expression of quiet melancholy. If there had been any Earthwomen on Damorlan, Clarey would have thought he'd been crossed in love.

"Things are taking a bad turn, Clarey," Blynn said. "There have been certain manifestations of hostility from the natives. Get any hint of it?"

"No," Clarey said, taking his usual chair, "not a whisper."

The colonel sat down heavily. "Katund's too out of the way. We should've moved you to a city once you'd got the feel of things. But you do go to Zrig occasionally. Haven't you heard anything there?"

"Only that an Earthman bought out a cloth merchant's entire stock at one blow."

Blynn grinned weakly. "Maybe it was rather an ostentatious thing to do, but the fabric's beautiful stuff."

He rubbed his nose reflectively. "Fact is, I've been hearing disturbing rumors. They say some fellow named Guhak's invented a ground car that can run without tracks."

Clarey almost said "Guhak," but caught himself in time. "Nonsense," he scoffed. "The more I know of them, the more surprised I am they ever got as far as inventing the chains."

"But they did, no getting around that. This is what Earth's afraid of, you know," he reminded Clarey unnecessarily. "This is why you were sent here. And, if the rumor's true, it looks as if you weren't needed at all. I got the bad news by myself."

"But why should it be that upsetting?" Clarey tried to laugh. "You look as if it were the end of the world."

The colonel gave him a long, level look. "I consider that remark in the worst of taste."

Clarey stopped laughing.

"Remember," the colonel reminded Clarey, again unnecessarily, "this is the way we ourselves got started."

"But the Damorlanti don't have to move in the same direction. They may look human and even act human, but they don't think human."

The colonel clasped his hands behind his head and sighed. "There have been articles against us in the paper, and whenever we go out in the street people—natives, I mean—make nasty remarks and sometimes even faces at us. And what have we done to them? Carefully minded our own business, avoided all cultural contacts except for trade purposes, paid them much more than the going price for their goods, and gave them one or two tips on health and sanitation. As a result, they're beginning to hate us."

"But if you send a report, it'll bring the staff ship in ahead of time. Maybe the whole thing'll blow over. This way, you're not giving it a chance to."

The colonel chewed his lip. "Well," he finally said, "I might as well wait and see if the rumor's verified before I report it."

CHAPTER FOUR

CLAREY went back to Katund. The months went by. The friendly atmosphere in the Furbush had vanished, and not as many people stopped and chatted when they came to the library. But there wasn't any actual incident until the evening Clarey was walking home after a late night at the library and a stone struck him between the shoulder blades. "Dirty Earthman!" a voice called, and several pairs of feet scuttled off.

He didn't mention the incident to Embelsira, not wanting to worry her, but the next morning he went to the Village Dome and informed Malesor. "Very bad," the headman muttered. *"Very* bad. Whoever did it will be punished."

"You won't be able to catch them," Clarey said, "and there'd be no point in punishment, anyway. Look at it like this, Mal. Suppose I had been an Earthman, don't you see how dangerous this would be, not for me but for you? Can't you imagine the inevitable results?"

Malesor nodded. "The Earthmen's catapults *do* go farther and faster, then?"

"And maybe deeper," Clarey agreed, pretending not to notice that it had been a question. "After the way Irik talked, I couldn't help drifting over to the starfield when I was in Barshwat and watching an Earth ship come. You've no idea how incredibly powerful a thing it was. Anyone who has power in one direction is likely to have it in another."

"I wonder if the Earthmen always had power," Malesor mused, "if they weren't like us once. If, given time, we couldn't be like them…"

Clarey didn't say anything.

Malesor's pale face turned gray. "You mean we might not be given time?"

Clarey wiggled his ears. "Who can tell what's in the mind of an Earthman?"

Malesor looked directly at him. "Why do you tell me this?"

"Because. I'm one of you," Clarey said stoutly.

Malesor shook his head. "You're not. You never can be. But thanks for the warning—stranger."

Never identify, the robocoach had said. *You'll never be able to become the character you're trying to play.* He was talking only of the stage, Clarey told himself angrily, as he left the Dome.

Reports trickled in from the cities. Earthmen had been stoned twice in Zrig, more often than that in Barshwat. Clarey got an agitated letter from his aunt. "Watch out for yourself, Nephew," she warned. "They may take it into their heads to attack all foreigners. Remember, come what may, you'll always have a home with me."

Then everything broke open. A group of natives attacked Earth Headquarters in Barshwat. The Earthmen sprayed them with a gas, which made the attackers lose consciousness without harming them; that is, it was intended to work that way. However, one of them hit his head on the wall when he fell, and he died the next day.

The people of Vintnor were aroused. They milled angrily around Earth Headquarters carrying banners that said, "Go home, Earth murderers!" The headman of Barshwat called upon Colonel Blynn. The colonel courteously refused to withdraw his men from the planet. "I'm under orders, old chap," he said, "but I'll report your request back to Earth."

"It isn't a request," the headman said.

Colonel Blynn smiled and said, "We'll treat it as one, shall we?"

Clarey knew what happened, because the headman gave a report of the conversation to the Barshwat Prime Bulletin. He also got a letter from his aunt describing the incident as vividly as if she had been there herself. The Barshwat Prime ran a series of increasingly intemperate editorials calling upon all the nations of Damorlan to unite against the Earthmen; it was spirit that counted, it said, rather than technology. Malesor wrote a letter asking how superior spiritual values could compete against presumably superior weapons. He read it aloud in the Purple Furbush before he sent it to the editor of the Barshwat Prime, which was lucky, because the Prime never printed it, although the Dordonec Bulletin ran a copy.

HOWEVER, the Barshwat Prime did print letters from editors in different countries. All of them pledged firm moral support. It also printed a letter from an anonymous correspondent in Katund, which alleged that there was an Earth spy in that village disguised as a Damorlant, and it was this spy who was personally responsible for the decline of musical taste on the whole planet. But the Bulletin seemed to consider this merely as an emanation from the lunatic fringe: "It would be as easy to disguise a hix as one of us as an Earthman. And, although we could certainly not minimize the importance of music in our culture, it is hardly likely that Earth would be attempting to achieve fell purposes through undermining that art. No, the decline in musical taste represents part of the general decline in public morality, which has left us an easy prey."

Irik went back to Barshwat to help riot, but he left the Katundi convinced that Clarey was, if not actually an Earthman, at least a traitor. When he came into the Furbush, everybody got up and left. Nobody patronized the branch library any more. The constant readers went to the main library at Zrig, and, since the trip was expensive, their books were usually overdue and they had to pay substantial fines. Sometimes they never returned the books at all and messengers had to be sent from the city. Finally the chief librarian at Zrig issued a regulation that only those resident within the city limits could take books out; all others in the district had to read them on the premises. The Katundi blamed that on Clarey, too. One night they broke into his library and stole all the bestsellers.

A couple of days later, he came home and found all the windows of his dome broken. Bestsellers are often disappointing, he thought. He found a note from Embelsira, saying, "I have gone home to Mother."

He knew she expected him to go after her, but he wrote her a note saying he was going to see his aunt who was terrified by all the riots, and put it in the mail, so she wouldn't get it too soon. He packed his kit with his most important possessions and he took his ulerin under his arm.

When he reached Barshwat, he had some difficulty getting through the crowd in front of Earth Headquarters. All the windows were boarded up and the garbage hadn't been collected for a considerable length of time. Just as he reached the door, a familiar voice called, "That's the Earth spy!"

"Don't be silly," another voice said. "He's obviously one of us."

"But a traitor," cried another voice. "Otherwise why go in there?" Stones splattered against the door, followed by impartial cries of, "Spy...! Traitor...! Fool...!" the last seemingly addressed to each other, rather than Clarey.

Blynn was haggard and anxious-looking. "I've been wondering when you'd show up. Afraid maybe they'd got you—"

"I'm all right," Clarey interrupted. "But what are we going to do?"

Blynn laughed without stopping for a full minute. "Do? I'll tell you what we're going to do. We're going to sit tight and wait for the staff ship."

Two months later the staff ship came. Blynn radioed for the general and the secretary to come in a closed ground car.

"But why?" the general's voice crackled plaintively over the com-unit. "I thought we didn't want them to know about ground cars—"

"They know," Blynn said crisply. "They've got one of their own now, maybe more. Crazy-looking thing, but it works. You'll see it outside Headquarters when you get here. The letters on the side mean 'Earthmen, Go!' Form imperative impolite emphatic."

Han Vollard strode into Headquarters, eyes ablaze. "Why didn't you send a report before trouble started? How could you allow an emergency situation to happen?"

Neither Blynn nor Carey said anything.

"Very distressing thing," Spano declared. "Maybe it hit them so suddenly they didn't know it was building."

"You and Blynn get over to the ship right away for deep-probing," Han Vollard ordered, as both began to speak at once. "It's the only way I'll be able to get a coherent report."

After the results came through, her anger was cold, searing, unwomanly. "You knew a year ago that things were beginning to go wrong and you didn't even *mention* it on the tapes. I could have both of you broken for this."

"If only that were all there was to worry about," Clarey sighed wistfully.

SHE WHIRLED on him. "Stop feeling sorry for yourself!" The sudden loss of control in that dark amazon was more threatening than anything that had happened yet.

"I'm not feeling sorry for myself," he said. "It's the Damorlanti I feel sorry for."

"You feel sorry for them because you identify with them. That makes you sorry for yourself."

She misunderstood his motives as she misunderstood everything he did or said, but their rapport wasn't at stake now. "What are you going to do?" he forced himself to ask.

"The decision will have to be made on Earth. Unless you mean what's going to happen to you? That's simple— you'll go back with us. Blynn will stay here, pending orders."

The colonel saluted.

"But I thought I was going to stay here ten years," said Clarey.

"Five to ten years," she corrected. "Apparently five was enough—" She cut herself short. "What's the matter with me?" she suddenly exclaimed. "I've been letting myself think in the same woolly way you do."

Suddenly, almost frighteningly, she smiled. "Clarey, you did the job we sent you out to do. You did it better than we expected. What threw me off was that we sent you out to act as an observer. Instead, you became a catalyst."

She seized his hand and wrung it warmly. "Clarey, I apologize. You've done a splendid job."

He wrenched his hand from her grasp. "I didn't act as a catalyst. It would have happened anyway." His voice rang in his own horrified ears—a voice begging for reassurance.

And she was a woman; she had maternal instincts; she reassured him. "It would have happened anyway," she said soothingly, "but it would have dragged on for years, cost the taxpayers billions."

"And now," he whispered, still unable to believe that the thing had really happened, "will you...dispose of everyone on Damorlan?"

She smiled and threw herself into a chair, her body limp and tired and contended-looking. "Come, Clarey, we're not that ruthless. Some kind of quarantine will probably be worked out. We just made the whole thing sound more drastic to appeal to your patriotism."

The general beamed. "So everything has worked out all right, after all? I knew it would. I always had the utmost confidence in you, Clarey."

She was busily planning. "We'll arrange some kind of heroic accident... I have it! You died saving your aunt from the flames."

"What flames?"

"The flames of the fire that burned down her house. She died of the local equivalent of shock. Embelsira will be rich, so she'll want to believe the story. She'll be able to find herself another husband; she'll have children. She'll be better off, Clarey."

He looked at her, his misery welling out of his eyes.

"Oh, I don't mean it that way, man. All I meant was that you're a human being; she's not. I'm not saying one is better than the other. I'm saying they're different."

"But I felt less different with her, with the Damorlanti, than with anyone on Earth," he said.

She walked across to the window and looked out at the Damorlanti rioting ineptly below. "Most of us are happier in our dream world," she said at last, "but society couldn't function if we were allowed to stay there."

"Damorlan wasn't a dream world."

"But it will be," she said.

CHAPTER FIVE

AND so Clarey went back to Earth on the staff ship. Once its luxury would have given him pleasure; now the cabin with its taps that gave out plain water, salt water, mineral water, and assorted cordials held no charm; neither did the self-contained tri-di projector-receiver. The only reason he stayed there most of the time was to avoid the others. However, he couldn't avoid turning up in the dining salon for meals. The greater his sorrow, the greater his appetite.

One day after lunch, Han stopped him forcibly, grasping his arm. "I've got to talk to you. Afterward you can go off and sulk if you want to. But we're going to make planet fall in a few days. It's necessary to discuss your future now."

"I have no future," he said.

"Come this way, Clarey. That's an order."

Obediently, he followed her into a lounge that was a dazzle of color and splendor. There were eight pseudo-windows, each framing a pseudo-scene of a different planet at a different season. The harsh, barren summer of Mars, the cold, bleak winter of Ksud, the gentle green spring of Earth... It must be a park, he knew in no other place on Earth could spring be manifest—and yet it gave him a little pang to look at it. He tore his eyes away to turn them toward the others, and then up at the domed ceiling, fashioned to resemble a blue sky with clouds drifting across it. A domed ceiling...and he thought of the domes of Damorlan, light-years away among the stars...

"I'm afraid the decor's a bit gaudy," Han apologized. "We didn't check the decorator's past performance until it was too late. But it's comfortable, anyway. Try one of these chairs. They accommodate themselves to the form."

She threw herself on a chaise lounge that accommodated itself perfectly to her form. She wasn't wearing her usual opulent secretarial garb, but something simple of clinging stuff that occasionally went transparent. So we're back to the first movement, Clarey though wearily.

He made sure that the chair opposite her was old-style before he lowered himself into it. "Where's the general? I thought he always sat in on these conferences."

"The formalities are over now," she said, smiling up at him. "Besides," she added, "if he doesn't take a nap after lunch, it wreaks havoc with his digestion. Afraid to be alone with me, Clarey?" she asked huskily.

"Yes," he said, rising, "as a matter of fact, I am, now that you mention it."

She sat up. "*Sit down.*"

He sat down.

She didn't recline again. Her dress went opaque, but her voice grew silken once more. "Listen, Clarey, I don't want you to think we're cheating you out of anything we promised. Even though you stayed only five years, you're going to have it all. You'll have U-E status—"

"What do I want that for?"

"Doesn't it mean anything to you any more, Clarey? It used to mean a lot, though you denied it even to yourself."

"Did it?" He forced his thoughts back through time. "I suppose it did. But I've changed. You know, those five years on Damorlan seem like—"

"Like a lifetime," she finished. "Couldn't we dispense with the cliches?"

"On Damorlan the things I said were fresh and interesting. On Damorlan I was somebody pretty special. I'd rather be a big second-hand fish in a small primitive puddle. Isn't there *some* way—"

"No way at all, Clarey. The puddle's drying up. We've got a nice aquarium ready for you. Why not dive in gracefully?"

"It was my puddle," he said. "I belonged."

SHE CLOSED her eyes and sank back into the chair, which arched to meet the arch of her body. Lying down, she didn't look nearly as tall. "All right, let's give the whole opera one final run-through. Nobody cared for you on Earth; on Damorlan your friends liked you; your wife loved you. On Earth you never felt welcome and/or appreciated; on Damorlan you felt both welcome and appreciated. On Earth—"

He was stung out of his apathy. "That's right... I'm not saying I'm unique, only that I fitted—"

"How about trying to look at it from another point of view? Did it ever occur to you that, if the Damorlanti accepted you, so might your own people, if you approached them in the same way? Did you ever *try* to make friends on Earth?"

"But on Earth I shouldn't have to. They were my own people."

"Aha!" she cried gleefully.

"I mean—well, General Spano said it would be wrong to stoop to hypocrisy to win the friendship of my own people; that, if I did, their friendship wouldn't be worth anything. You can't buy friendship."

"You bought your ulerin. Does it play any the worse because you paid for it? Does it mean any the less to you?"

"What you're getting at," he said cautiously, "is that that's the way to make friends? By being a hypocrite?"

"Was it a sham with the Damorlanti?"

He had to stop for a moment before he could bring out an answer. "It started out as a sham—but I really got to like them afterward. Then it was real."

"So then you weren't a hypocrite, Clarey." Her voice grew more resonant. "Open yourself to people, show them that you want to be friends. Basically, everybody's shy and timid inside."

"Like you?" he said, casting an ironical glance at her dress.

"That's still the outside," she smiled, making, no move to adjust it. "Listen to me, Clarey, and don't go off on sidetracks: The people of Earth are your own people. Your loyalties have always been with them."

She had almost had him convinced, but this he couldn't swallow. "If my loyalties had been with Earth, I would have sent back reports of the trouble. But I didn't. I tried to stop it from happening. There just wasn't anything I could do."

"The deep-probe never lies, Clarey. You didn't really try to stop it." She paused, and then went on deliberately: "Because you could have stopped it, you know quite easily."

"There was nothing I could have done," he stated. "Nothing."

"Remember the first time the staff ship came? Just before you left for Barshwat, the woman told you she suspected you were an Earthman. You were afraid for her. Do you remember that?"

He nodded. Yes, he remembered how terrified he had been then, how relieved afterward, thinking everything was going to be all right. Lucky he hadn't realized the truth, or he wouldn't have had those extra years of happiness.

HAN WENT on remorselessly: "And you thought if only something would happen to you en route, she would be safe. We might guess why it had happened, but we couldn't know for sure. We'd have had to start all over again."

He couldn't move, couldn't speak, couldn't think. She spaced each word carefully, sweetly. "You were quite right. Because you were the only man on Earth, Clarey, who had the particular physical requirements and the particular kind of mental instability that we needed for the job. You just said you weren't unique, Clarey. You were too modest; you are. If you'd killed yourself then, your death would have served a purpose; you would have died a hero. Kill yourself now and you die a coward."

"But at least I'd be dead. I wouldn't have to live with a coward for the rest of my life."

"You're not a coward, Clarey," she said. "You wouldn't admit it, but you are and always have been a patriot. To you, Earth came first. It's as simple as that."

She had deep-probed his mind. She must know his true feelings. There was no gainsaying that. He could know only his surface thoughts; she knew what lay behind and beneath. And, he reminded himself, at the end the Damorlanti were actually turning on him.

"Try to think of the whole thing as a course in charm that you've passed with flying colors," she said.

"It seems rather an expensive way of making me charming," he couldn't help saying, with the last struggle of something that was dying in him, something alien that perhaps should never have been there in the first place.

"Whole civilizations have been sacrificed for nothing at all. This one will not be sacrificed, only quarantined. But its contribution could be of cosmic magnitude."

"Now what are you going to try to sell me?" he asked drearily. "Are you saying that the essence of the Damorlant civilization is going to live on in me, that I carry its heritage inside myself, and so I have a tremendous responsibility to the Damorlanti on my shoulders?"

She laughed. "You're really getting sharp, Clarey. If you stayed in the service, you could be one of our best operatives. But you're not going to stay in the service. Yours is a higher destiny. Here, catch…"

She tossed him something that glittered as it arched through the air.

It was a U-E identcube, made out in his name. He had only seen them at a distance, and now he was holding one warm and gleaming in his hand, with his name and his face in it. His face…and yet not his face.

"That's what you're going to look like when the plastosurgeons get through," she explained. "They'll pigment your eyes and skin and hair, and they may be able to add a few inches to your height. Though I think you actually have grown a little. Something about the air, or, more likely, the food."

"Embelsira thought I was handsome the way I was. Embelsira…" But Embelsira was light-years away. Embelsira was part of a fading dream—and he was awakening now to reality.

"Look at the cube. Look at your status symbol."

He looked at it, and he kept on looking at it. He couldn't tear his eyes away. He was hypnotized by the golden glitter of it, the golden meaning of it. "Musician," he said aloud. "Musician…" A dream word, a magic word. He hadn't thought of it for years; but this he didn't have to reach back for. Once touched on, it surged over him, complete with its memories.

BUT SHE had made it meaningless, too. He managed to tear a laugh out of his throat. "Spano said I'd be able to buy the Musicians' Guild when I had my million and a half. Apparently you've been able to bargain them down."

"This cost nothing except the standard initiation fee," she told him. "You came by it honestly—through your music, nothing else. And you have more than a million and a half credits, Clarey—nearly ten times that, with more pouring in every day."

She touched a boss on the side of her chair and white light hazed around them. "I think we're close enough to Earth to get some of the high-power tri-dis," she said, "although we can't expect perfect reception."

Blurrily, a show formed—a variety show. At first it seemed the same sort of thing that he remembered dimly, more interesting now because it had almost the character of novelty. Then an ornate young man appeared and it took deeper significance. He was carrying a musical instrument—refined, machined, carefully pitched. He played music on the ulerin while a trio sang insipid Terrestrial words. "Love Is a Guiding Star" they called it, but that didn't matter. It was one of the tunes Clarey had taped.

She touched another boss. The blur reformed to a symphony orchestra, playing as background music to a soloist with another ulerin. "That's your First Ulerin Concerto," she said. "There are three more."

Another program was beginning, an account of the tribulations of an unfortunate Plutonian family. It faded into the strains of ulerin music, to a tune of Clarey's. If they could have endured it to the end, she told him, it would have faded out the same way. "Every time they play it," she said, "somewhere on Earth a cash register rings for you. And this one's a daily program."

He watched transfixed and transfigured as program after program featured his music, his ulerin.

"Not just on Earth," Han said, "but on all the civilized planets, even in a few of the more sophisticated primitive ones. You're a famous man, Clarey. Earth is waiting for you, literally and figuratively. There'll be ulerin orchestras to greet you at the field; we sent a relay ahead to let them know you were coming."

But his mind was slowly alerting itself. "And where am I supposed to be coming from, then, since they're never to hear about Damorlan?"

"They've been told that you retired to a lonely asteroid to work—to perfect your art and its instrument."

Of course they couldn't divulge the truth about Damorlan. "It seems a little unfair, though," he said.

"Why unfair? After all, Clarey, the music is yours. You took Damorlan's melodies and made them into music. You took their ulerin and made it into a musical instrument. They're all yours, every note and bladder of them."

She reached over and put out a hand to him. "And I'm yours, too, Clarey, if you want me," she breathed. There was obviously no doubt in her mind that he did want her. And in his, too. One didn't reject the Secretary of Space.

He took the chilly hand in his. The skin was odd in texture. I'm imagining things, he thought. It's a long time since I touched a human female's hand.

"I must be a very important Musician," he said aloud.

SHE NODDED, not pretending to misunderstand. "Yes, important enough to rate the original and not a reasonable facsimile. You're a lucky man, Clarey." And then she smiled up at him. "I can be warm and tender, I assure you."

It took him a moment to realize what she meant. For a moment he had that pang again. She would never be the same as Embelsira, but a man needed change to develop.

He was still troubled, though. "I want to do *something*. Even an empty gesture's better than none at all. The last few months, I started putting together a longer thing; I guess it could be a symphony. When I finish it, I'd like to call it the 'Damorlant Symphony.'"

"Why not?" she said. He thought she was humoring him, but she added, "They'll think you just picked the name from an astrogation chart."

In a final burst of irony he dedicated the "Damorlant Symphony" to the human race, but, as usual, he was misunderstood. In fact, one of the music critics—all of whom were enthusiastic over the new work wrote, "At last we have a great musician who is also a great humanist."

Eventually Clarey forgot his original intent and came to believe it himself.

THE END

If you've enjoyed this book, you will not want to miss these terrific titles...

ARMCHAIR SCI-FI & HORROR DOUBLE NOVELS, $12.95 each

D-1   **THE GALAXY RAIDERS** by William P. McGivern
           SPACE STATION #1 by Frank Belknap Long

D-2   **THE PROGRAMMED PEOPLE** by Jack Sharkey
           SLAVES OF THE CRYSTAL BRAIN by William Carter Sawtelle

D-3   **YOU'RE ALL ALONE** by Fritz Leiber
           THE LIQUID MAN by Bernard C. Gilford

D-4   **CITADEL OF THE STAR LORDS** by Edmond Hamilton
           VOYAGE TO ETERNITY by Milton Lesser

D-5   **IRON MEN OF VENUS** by Don Wilcox
           THE MAN WITH ABSOLUTE MOTION by Noel Loomis

D-6   **WHO SOWS THE WIND...** by Rog Phillips
           THE PUZZLE PLANET by Robert A. W. Lowndes

D-7   **PLANET OF DREAD** by Murray Leinster
           TWICE UPON A TIME by Charles L. Fontenay

D-8   **THE TERROR OUT OF SPACE** by Dwight V. Swain
           QUEST OF THE GOLDEN APE by Paul W. Fairman & Milton Lesser

D-9   **SECRET OF MARRACOTT DEEP** by Henry Slesar
           PAWN OF THE BLACK FLEET by Mark Clifton.

D-10   **BEYOND THE RINGS OF SATURN** by Robert Moore Williams
           A MAN OBSESSED by Alan E. Nourse

ARMCHAIR SCIENCE FICTION CLASSICS, $12.95 each

C-1   **THE GREEN MAN**
           by Harold M. Sherman

C-2   **A TRACE OF MEMORY**
           By Keith Laumer

C-3   **INTO PLUTONIAN DEPTHS**
           by Stanton A. Coblentz

ARMCHAIR MASTERS OF SCIENCE FICTION SERIES, $16.95 each

M-1   **MASTERS OF SCIENCE FICTION, Vol. One**
           Bryce Walton—"Dark of the Moon" and other tales

M-2   **MASTERS OF SCIENCE FICTION, Vol. Two**
           Jerome Bixby—"One Way Street" and other tales

If you've enjoyed this book, you will not want to miss these terrific titles…

ARMCHAIR SCI-FI & HORROR DOUBLE NOVELS, $12.95 each

D-11   **PERIL OF THE STARMEN** by Kris Neville
       THE STRANGE INVASION by Murray Leinster

D-12   **THE STAR LORD** by Boyd Ellanby
       CAPTIVES OF THE FLAME by Samuel R. Delany

D-13   **MEN OF THE MORNING STAR** by Edmond Hamilton
       PLANET FOR PLUNDER by Hal Clement and Sam Merwin, Jr.

D-14   **ICE CITY OF THE GORGON** by Chester S. Geier and Richard Shaver
       WHEN THE WORLD TOTTERED by Lester del Rey

D-15   **WORLDS WITHOUT END** by Clifford D. Simak
       THE LAVENDER VINE OF DEATH by Don Wilcox

D-16   **SHADOW ON THE MOON** by Joe Gibson
       ARMAGEDDON EARTH by Geoff St. Reynard

D-17   **THE GIRL WHO LOVED DEATH** by Paul W. Fairman
       SLAVE PLANET by Laurence M. Janifer

D-18   **SECOND CHANCE** by J. F. Bone
       MISSION TO A DISTANT STAR by Frank Belknap Long

D-19   **THE SYNDIC** by C. M. Kornbluth
       FLIGHT TO FOREVER by Poul Anderson

D-20   **SOMEWHERE I'LL FIND YOU** by Milton Lesser
       THE TIME ARMADA by Fox B. Holden

ARMCHAIR SCIENCE FICTION CLASSICS, $12.95 each

C-4   **CORPUS EARTHLING**
       by Louis Charbonneau

C-5   **THE TIME DISSOLVER**
       by Jerry Sohl

C-6   **WEST OF THE SUN**
       by Edgar Pangborn

ARMCHAIR SCI-FI & HORROR GEMS SERIES, $12.95 each

G-1   **SCIENCE FICTION GEMS, Vol. One**
       Isaac Asimov and others

G-2   **HORROR GEMS, Vol. One**
       Carl Jacobi and others

If you've enjoyed this book, you will not want to miss these terrific titles…

ARMCHAIR SCI-FI & HORROR DOUBLE NOVELS, $12.95 each

D-21   **EMPIRE OF EVIL** by Robert Arnette
THE SIGN OF THE TIGER by Alan E. Nourse & J. A. Meyer

D-22   **OPERATION SQUARE PEG** by Frank Belknap Long
ENCHANTRESS OF VENUS by Leigh Brackett

D-23   **THE LIFE WATCH** by Lester del Rey
CREATURES OF THE ABYSS by Murray Leinster

D-24   **LEGION OF LAZARUS** by Edmond Hamilton
STAR HUNTER by Andre Norton

D-25   **EMPIRE OF WOMEN** by John Fletcher
ONE OF OUR CITIES IS MISSING by Irving Cox

D-26   **THE WRONG SIDE OF PARADISE** by Raymond F. Jones
THE INVOLUNTARY IMMORTALS by Rog Phillips

D-27   **EARTH QUARTER** by Damon Knight
ENVOY TO NEW WORLDS by Keith Laumer

D-28   **SLAVES TO THE METAL HORDE** by Milton Lesser
HUNTERS OUT OF TIME by Joseph E. Kelleam

D-29   **RX JUPITER SAVE US** by Ward Moore
BEWARE THE USURPERS by Geoff St. Reynard

D-30   **SECRET OF THE SERPENT** by Don Wilcox
CRUSADE ACROSS THE VOID by Dwight V. Swain

ARMCHAIR SCIENCE FICTION CLASSICS, $12.95 each

C-7   **THE SHAVER MYSTERY, Book One**
by Richard S. Shaver

C-8   **THE SHAVER MYSTERY, Book Two**
by Richard S. Shaver

C-9   **MURDER IN SPACE**
by David V. Reed

ARMCHAIR MASTERS OF SCIENCE FICTION SERIES, $16.95 each

M-3   **MASTERS OF SCIENCE FICTION, Vol. Three**
Robert Sheckley, "The Perfect Woman" and other tales

M-4   **MASTERS OF SCIENCE FICTION, Vol. Four**
Mack Reynolds, Part One, "Stowaway" and other tales

If you've enjoyed this book, you will not want to miss these terrific titles…

ARMCHAIR SCI-FI & HORROR DOUBLE NOVELS, $12.95 each

D-31 **A HOAX IN TIME** by Keith Laumer
     INSIDE EARTH by Poul Anderson

D-32 **TERROR STATION** by Dwight V. Swain
     THE WEAPON FROM ETERNITY by Dwight V. Swain

D-33 **THE SHIP FROM INFINITY** by Edmond Hamilton
     TAKEOFF by C. M. Kornbluth

D-34 **THE METAL DOOM** by David H. Keller
     TWELVE TIMES ZERO by Howard Browne

D-35 **HUNTERS OUT OF SPACE** by Joseph Kelleam
     INVASION FROM THE DEEP by Paul W. Fairman,

D-36 **THE BEES OF DEATH** by Robert Moore Williams
     A PLAGUE OF PYTHONS by Frederik Pohl

D-37 **THE LORDS OF QUARMALL** by Fritz Leiber and Harry Fischer
     BEACON TO ELSEWHERE by James H. Schmitz

D-38 **BEYOND PLUTO** by John S. Campbell
     ARTERY OF FIRE by Thomas N. Scortia

D-39 **SPECIAL DELIVERY** by Kris Neville
     NO TIME FOR TOFFEE by Charles F. Meyers

D-40 **JUNGLE IN THE SKY** by Milton Lesser
     RECALLED TO LIFE by Robert Silverberg

ARMCHAIR SCIENCE FICTION CLASSICS, $12.95 each

C-10 **MARS IS MY DESTINATION**
     by Frank Belknap Long

C-11 **SPACE PLAGUE**
     by George O. Smith

C-12 **SO SHALL YE REAP**
     by Rog Phillips

ARMCHAIR SCI-FI & HORROR GEMS SERIES, $12.95 each

G-3 **SCIENCE FICTION GEMS, Vol. Two**
    James Blish and others

G-4 **HORROR GEMS, Vol. Two**
    Joseph Payne Brennan and others

If you've enjoyed this book, you will not want to miss these terrific titles…

ARMCHAIR SCI-FI & HORROR DOUBLE NOVELS, $12.95 each

D-41 **FULL CYCLE** by Clifford D. Simak
IT WAS THE DAY OF THE ROBOT by Frank Belknap Long

D-42 **THIS CROWDED EARTH** by Robert Bloch
REIGN OF THE TELEPUPPETS by Daniel Galouye

D-43 **THE CRISPIN AFFAIR** by Jack Sharkey
THE RED HELL OF JUPITER by Paul Ernst

D-44 **PLANET OF DREAD** by Dwight V. Swain
WE THE MACHINE by Gerald Vance

D-45 **THE STAR HUNTER** by Edmond Hamilton
THE ALIEN by Raymond F. Jones

D-46 **WORLD OF IF** by Rog Phillips
SLAVE RAIDERS FROM MERCURY by Don Wilcox

D-47 **THE ULTIMATE PERIL** by Robert Abernathy
PLANET OF SHAME by Bruce Elliot

D-48 **THE FLYING EYES** by J. Hunter Holly
SOME FABULOUS YONDER by Phillip Jose Farmer

D-49 **THE COSMIC BUNGLERS** by Geoff St. Reynard
THE BUTTONED SKY by Geoff St. Reynard

D-50 **TYRANTS OF TIME** by Milton Lesser
PARIAH PLANET by Murray Leinster

ARMCHAIR SCIENCE FICTION CLASSICS, $12.95 each

C-13 **SUNKEN WORLD**
by Stanton A. Coblentz

C-14 **THE LAST VIAL**
by Sam McClatchie, M. D.

C-15 **WE WHO SURVIVED (THE FIFTH ICE AGE)**
by Sterling Noel

ARMCHAIR MASTERS OF SCIENCE FICTION SERIES, $16.95 each

MS-5 **MASTERS OF SCIENCE FICTION, Vol. Five**
Winston K. Marks—Test Colony and other tales

MS-6 **MASTERS OF SCIENCE FICTION, Vol. Six**
Fritz Leiber—Deadly Moon and other tales

If you've enjoyed this book, you will not want to miss these terrific titles…

ARMCHAIR SCI-FI & HORROR DOUBLE NOVELS, $12.95 each

D-111   **THE MOON ERA** by Jack Williamson
        REVENGE OF THE ROBOTS by Howard Browne

D-112   **SON OF THE BLACK CHALICE** by Milton Lesser
        SENTRY OF THE SKY by Evelyn E. Smith

D-113   **OUTPOST ON THE MOON** by Joslyn Maxwell
        POTENTIAL ZERO by S. J. Byrne

D-114   **OUTPOST INFINITY** by Raymond F. Jones
        THE WHITE INVADERS by Ray Cummings

D-115   **TIME TRAP** by Rog Phillips
        THE COSMIC DESTROYER by Alexander Blade

D-116   **THE OTHER SIDE OF THE MOON** by Edmond Hamilton
        SECRET INVASION by Walter Kubilius

D-117   **DANGER MOON** by Frederik Pohl
        THE HIDDEN UNIVERSE by Ralph Milne Farley

D-118   **THE WAILING ASTEROID** by Murray Leinster
        THE WORLD THAT COULDN'T BE by Clifford D. Simak

D-119   **THE WHISPERING GORILLA** by Don Wilcox
        RETURN OF THE WHISPERING GORILLA by David V. Reed

D-120   **SPECIAL EFFECT** by J. F. Bone
        WARLORD OF KOR by Terry Carr

ARMCHAIR SCIENCE FICTION CLASSICS, $12.95 each

C-37   **THE GREEN MAN RETURNS**
       by Harold M. Sherman

C-38   **THE SHAVER MYSTERY, Book Five**
       by Richard S, Shaver

C-39   **MARS CHILD**
       by Cyril Judd

ARMCHAIR MASTERS OF SCIENCE FICTION SERIES, $16.95 each

MS-9   **MASTERS OF SCIENCE FICTION AND FANTASY, Vol. Nine**
       Poul Anderson, "The Star Beast" and other tales

MS-10   **MASTERS OF SCIENCE FICTION, Vol. Ten**
       Robert Moore Williams, "Time Tolls for Toro" and other tales